Julie and Jim

ALSO BY LEO BIRCH

Angelica

Seven Stories

Julie and Jim

A SENSUAL ROMANCE

Leo Birch

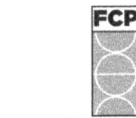

Full Court Press
Englewood Cliffs, New Jersey

First Edition

Copyright © 2024 by Leo Birch

Published in the United States of America
by Full Court Press, 601 Palisade Avenue,
Englewood Cliffs, NJ 07632
fullcourtpress.com

PRINT ISBN 978-1-953728-27-2
EBOOK ISBN 978-1-953728-28-9
Library of Congress Control No. 2024903732

Editing and book design by Barry Sheinkopf

TO NINA

PREFACE: NINA'S TREE

MY MOTHER USED TO SAY the hours before midnight count double. She said that a long time ago, when the hours did count for her.

I run several mornings a week with my friend Roy. We run at sunrise, around the loop of asphalt that unfolds ahead of us in Central Park in New York City. We run for the fun of it. For the talk, for the fitness. And we run ahead of the decades that follow us. These runs count double for me.

I love getting them done early, sometimes even going back to bed after. Later in the day, I'd tell myself, "I have to work out," and then, blissfully, I remember that have already!

When his father, the sweetest of man, passed away, Roy dedicated a colossal oak tree along our running route to his memory. Every time we run by, we greet him, and Roy reads the message his father sent him from years of love through the great trunk and limbs and leaves of that tree.

We both wave. And the run goes on.

My wife, Nina, whom I started loving when she was in her early twenties, died at fifty-seven, five years ago. It made sense we should find a tree for her as well. Roy pointed once to hi-saalong the West Side. It has an umbrella-like cropped canopy high up above a long cylinder of a trunk. I had always liked that tree. It always stood out, even after countless loops and endless miles of multiple past marathon-training runs. So I kept it in mind.

Eventually, over time, we started modifying our running routine route. We now stopped by a giant egg-shaped rock that sprouted out in a meadow by the playing fields where I used to play soccer when I first met Nina. I remember her coming to see one of my pick-up games. I was a shirtless, young, sweaty punk, and she came to the edge of the field on the horse she rode on Sundays in the park, at a time when they still allowed that.

All the players looked at her. She smiled, waved, and let the game go on.

The egg-shaped rock is made of granite. It is a visible clue to the solid bedrock that allowed Manhattan to support its tall buildings. Roy and I stand on it for a moment of silence before we finish the last three miles. We also started to cut left from West to East shortly after the cinder trail of the reservoir. And there, I found the tree for Nina. Actually, it is a group of trees.

Pine trees lodged in a circular enclave contained by a low simple wooden fence. Like the fences you see out at the beach, with two roughly cut trunks linked by posts. The pines, there must be a dozen of them, are almost an anomaly in that part of the park where most trees are deciduous. The outer pines all seem to lean gracefully towards a tall and healthy central one.

None of the trees are Nina. All of the trees are Nina.

I was riding the bike super-early with my other friend Eddie. I told him the story of the trees. "So what is the isolated pine tree for?" he asked.

"It's her pussy," I answered, as I smiled at it on the way up the steady hill.

ONE

THE GREEN DUCK GLIDING ON THE WATER had been waiting for her. Or maybe it was the sun that had been waiting for her. The sun that rose lazily that day, right in the axis of the Manhattan Street grid, as it does only a few days each year as if a giant hand had rotated the city's profile along a dial and adjusted it so perfectly that the orange flare of early morning light could spread itself evenly through the streets.

She was aware of both of them, the duck and the sun, as she rounded her loop of Central Park. She was almost done with her run. All she had left to run was the half mile from the West Side back to 5th Avenue. *Maybe it's a mallard*, she thought as she continued along 72nd Street.

The duck paddled along the surface of the lake that links

the John Lennon Memorial to the Bethesda Terrace. She *had* to stop and watch it. It was just too perfect! The delicate Art Box Bridge stood as a romantic backdrop to the small creature as it was forging alone along the sunrise's orange and crimson shimmer, leaving in its wake an expanding ripple of dark water.

She got closer to the fence surrounding the lake, held on to the railing, and slowly lowered her body toward the ground. From this vantage, she could see the water behind the moving duck forming a giant V, one limb moving towards her and the other towards the bridge. In her mind, she could actually feel the extension of the limb moving toward her and pass right hrough her. Right through her body. Caressing it. All of it—its smoothness reminding her of the hand of her loving husband.

The duck glided inexorably away, and she stood up again, feeling the pull on her legs, right there, by her inner thighs, where the warmth had accumulated.

She started running toward home and passed the sculpture by the Bethesda fountain. It had been designed by a woman and was also the city's first major commission awarded to a woman. She liked that little trivia. She slowed her pace, smiled at the Angel, and as usual, it smiled back. Now, her day could really begin.

She took one last look at the surface of the lake. The water was disturbed by rays of narrow light and ripples from other birds and thrown pebbles. She had to take another glance. She thought she had seen him, there on the surface—his face. Just for a moment, and then it was gone. Like he was gone. He kept coming back, though. She knew he tried.

Sometimes, she would see him everywhere, even in the egg cups. She was cleaning one just then under a stream of hot water in the kitchen, with the yolk from that morning's breakfast still clinging to it. They had liked the cups so much when they vacationed in Prague that they bought four of them and had to schlep them halfway across the world. She let her long fingers linger a bit longer on the smooth shape, finding comfort in the holes and crevices, playing with it under the warm soapy water. She could get romantic about such things. Almost a year ago, he was slipping away between her fingers, like the ceramic holder was doing now. His strong body withered away without a sound, without a crack. With nothing to prepare her. Just like that. He just slipped away one day. Soundlessly. And since the day he was gone, time itself had left. Only the present remained.

With her hands under the stream of warm water, she continued to play a game with his shape. He had not died. She had. There was no lying about it. Leaving seemed a lot easier than living. She cleaned the second egg holder much faster. There was work to do.

TWO

JULIE WAS FAIRLY TALL AT FIVE FOOT TEN. She had cropped her long auburn hair after Henry died. That turned out not to be a bad idea. Recently, her hair had started turning gray though she was only forty-four. She was OK with it, though. There's a look here, she told herself in the mornings as she looked at her own reflection in the mirror. Her Dutch mother had given her the sharp features, and from her father she'd gotten the darker Mediterranean complexion. She felt as if she belonged to neither ethnic group. She defined herself as singular and, as such, believed she owed nothing to anybody. She'd managed to remain independent when she lived with her husband and now was even more fiercely so, to the despair of her family and friends. She loved them all, but what she really wanted was room to breathe. Alone.

She was a photographer. She had wanted to make a career out of being a fine art photographer like Cindy Sherman, but life being what it is, she'd ended up becoming a fashion photographer instead. And a pretty good one at that! She had done the old-fashioned photo shoots, traveling with a crew and loads of equipment. It would take them, at that time, a few days to get the five or six shots the magazine required, but it was altogether fun. Now they did it all in two days max, sometimes not even on location. The fun was mostly gone. That had become true for so many things in life. Everything was efficient now, digitized and enhanced, faster and diluted, and no one said anything about it. It all got accepted in the name of progress and then infused to the next generations, who saw no difference. It became the new norm. It didn't really affect her, or at least she didn't pay too much attention to it. She was too busy trying not to get diluted by the flow of time.

Today could be painful. Even though it had been almost a year now, each day carried its own weight in memories. Each geographical place too, even each person. All of these had the power to take her back. There was no escape from grief except in the full embrace of the present. Living in the moment left no room for grief, she had quickly found out, that moment being just too full for anything else, like a silver cup filled to the brim.

HER NEW ADVENTURE STARTED as a concept that formed in her head while she looked at picture albums several months after

Henry had passed. There were many images of them together, selfies and others, in all states of life and fun and pleasure, but there were none of them truly together. Of them naked and close, naked and kissing, naked and smiling, just as they always did. No pictures, when she came to think about it, of either him or her completely naked or at least scantily clad. It had never occurred to them at that time. There was no need. There was always tomorrow. Until there was no morning following the last one, and all the images that could have been were gone, and not even forgotten. Her business concept was to allow people to experience what she couldn't. She would provide them with a memento to look at, not only in death, but also in health, and in fun, and perhaps even in lust. So she came up with the idea of photographing people in their own homes. They would show up in teams of two. Always a man and a woman, a team that would take pictures while ensuring the subjects were comfortable. The subjects would always own the images after the shoot, either on a roll of film or on a digital memory card. The whole enterprise remained only a concept for the time being, but it kept her mind busy, and she needed that.

That day, she had a business meeting scheduled. She was going to meet a young photographer recommended by a mutual friend. The friend was not too sure what kind of individual she was really looking for, but then again, neither was she. The guy she was going to meet was called Jim, which kind of made

her smile already. Her name was Julie. If they worked together, they would be "Julie and Jim." Almost like *Jules et
Jim,* the classic movie—another icon that no longer existed.
Unless I do a remake, she was thinking as she entered Lu-
cien, the small French restaurant where they were scheduled
to meet.

Julie had been told that Jim was twenty-seven and had
worked as a model when he was younger, when the media
wanted men who looked manly like he did. But now, the new
wave wanted men who looked like the new era, and he was no
longer being solicited. Jim was OK with that, for he had always wanted to switch to the other side of the camera anyway,
and according to his acquaintance, this meeting with Julie
might open such possibilities.

She knew it was him as soon as he entered the restaurant.
He had wavy brown hair that he kept short, yet it managed to
look unruly. She found him seriously good-looking.

He was curious. She was a little nervous. They sat down
at a table, strangely enough, side by side. Across the room was
a mirror, and they could see each other that way. It was a prelude to their future.

She explained to him in a few sentences the outlines of her
plan.

"So we'd go to their houses and take pictures. Of them?
In their intimacy?" he asked.

"Yes," she said, "exactly. We would capture the moments

that no one dares to show."

"Why would anyone do this?"

"Well, because now, everything needs to be recorded and documented. Even shared sometimes," she said. "At first, we'll make it possible for just a few people. And then they'll show it to their friends. Hopefully, in turn, they too will want it."

"And then. . .we have a business?"

"Yes, exactly. People will ask, "Did you get your picture taken by the two photographers?"

"Did you get *Julie and Jimmed*?" he added excitedly.

"Perfect! Actually, *J & Jed*!"

"Done!" he said. "I'm in!"

AND JUST LIKE THAT, OVER A WARM TARTE TATIN, they shook hands, watching the celebration of their new venture in the reflection of the mirrored wall.

THREE

W HAT'S NEXT?" HE HAD ASKED after that meeting. She explained to him that the next step was
to spend some time in her studio to better understand how they could work harmoniously together.

She still kept a studio, though she rarely used it these days.
It was a reminder of what life as an artist was and of photographs taken in the spirit of creating transcendent images. Julie
believed that photographs usually failed to enhance their subjects at the instant of capture for, most often, they would
barely scratch the surface of the subject's beauty. On the other
hand, when a picture reveals itself from the inside out, un-
curling itself from somewhere deep and spreading itself along
the surface of the paper or the screen, then at last it reaches
the maturity of an art form. She saw the whole world that

same way lately—as a large windowpane against which all pressed their faces, their lives, waiting to get through, urging the glass to melt and let them appear around her. She kept them at bay. What she had now, the life she had created around her, was good enough.

She took the first few pictures to familiarize Jim with the different cameras she had. She used a variety of them, starting with an old Polaroid, watchful of the amount of film she used since it was vintage now and disappearing fast. Then there was the Hasselblad, the Contax, and a handful of different compact digital units.

They took turns taking pictures. It was clear that she was going to take the lead when it came to the first client photo-shoots. He was there to be part of the team, though, with the whole concept being that, faced with both a man and a woman, the client would have no fear of either being judged or assaulted.

Julie and Jim. She liked the ring of it. And he's turning out to be a sweetheart, she thought: helpful without being obsequious and manly enough to project strength and confidence. And for her, the best thing about him was his laugh. It echoed loud and clear when he let it ring, and as such it was also contagious. Whatever was funny enough to make him laugh became even funnier when you listened to his laughter.

Jim was learning a lot about photography with Julie, and he valued that. He wanted nothing else at that moment but to learn and be carried along the path of something new and relevant. He was far away from the home he had grown up in and the days of chopping wood for the heating stove. He had learned much from traveling with photo crews and meeting crowds so different from friends back home. At first, most people considered him a bit of an alien with his country ways, and he used his laugh as a form of defense. Now, the same laugh had become his strength, and he knew it. He also knew himself better. He was maturing, just like the Polaroid image Julie had taken, which was gradually developing in front of his eyes. He looked fantastically naked in the photo, hidden and exposed at once. He saw the power of her gaze, her hands. She had a way about her that seemed personal yet universal. She had photographed him as if he were a flower twisted upon itself, revealing nothing, but still showing everything. He kept that picture in his wallet.

"Why am I doing this?" Julie thought out loud as she got back home that night. "Am I opening a can of worms?" There was doubt and an ill feeling about the whole venture. What had started as a mere concept, the shadow of an idea, was slowly materializing. She even had her first client! She'd told a few of her friends about the project, not to solicit their business but to ask for possible leads, and now she was booked. "*We* are booked," she reminded herself.

They were to shoot a woman. Julie knew little about her— only that she had her own place in Soho and wanted a portrait.

The lack of information suited Julie. She wanted to know as little as possible about her subjects. She wouldn't research them on the internet or ask other people about them. When she went to do a photo shoot, she wanted to experience the full impact of the moment when she met her subject for the first time. It was, in her mind, an instance easily discounted by most yet pregnant with future ramifications. She valued each aspect of the encounter. From the first glance of previously unfamiliar eyes to the meeting of foreign hands, at which moment one briefly joins past personal histories. She wanted her photographs to be analogous to a handshake. A quick connection that could jump-start life in so many unusual ways.

The day of the shoot she had her morning tea before sunrise, early as usual. The client had requested a morning shoot. Something about the light, she had said. Jim had already texted Julie that he was on his way over to pick her up.

FOUR

S HE PACKED HER CAMERAS in the back of the car, checked her pockets for her phone, and smiled when she found, somehow lodged deep in the side pocket of her loose pants, the still-warm spoon she used to pour honey in her tea. Back in her kitchen, standing by the counter, she would stir her tea with that spoon, letting the weight of the honey find its way to the bottom of the mug so that the last sip became the sweetest. A joyful metaphor for life, she always thought. Objects, like this spoon, do become alive when attention is paid to them, and when this happens, it can become a very private and intimate affair. This is especially true for mundane objects, like a favorite cup, or a pen, or even a steering wheel.

She ended up keeping the spoon in her pocket, and from then on she carried it with her like a talisman of sorts on every new photo shoot. Even now she held on to it as she chatted with Jim all the way downtown to Soho.

They arrived at the loft with the sun barely making its way past the flat tar roofs of the nearby buildings. The apartment was on the top floor, with windows facing both east and west. The main room was a large expanse of empty space supported by columns rather than walls. The woman explained to them that she only stayed there a few nights a month. She pointed to a room in a corner, the only walled-in space, centered on one of the large west windows. "I sleep there when the sun sets right," she said. "I like to think of it as my private 'Turrell space.'" There was a smaller room next to it. "The bathroom," she hinted.

An armoire by Prouvé was the only closet space, and in an angle by the east windows was a built-in kitchen with a metallic sink lodged deep within a thick slab of wood. "I mainly eat out," she said, "or take in." She smiled, as if realizing what her words could mean. She watched Jim as he casually ran his hands along the rim of the kitchen counter, feeling the thickness of the wood and its smooth edge.

Her name was Chloe. She had beautiful long legs, tanned from a recent winter trip. "In the islands," she said. Saint Barths, thought Julie, hearing the hint of a French accent and also thinking it was classy of the woman not to mention it by name. She wore shorts made of a synthetic light gray material with a pink trim around the edge. They fit her perfectly, as if they were customized, which, based on everything else around her, seemed very possible. They were loose at the bottom and fastened to her narrow waist by a single, flat, dark gray cord.

"Almost like a miniature boxing outfit," said Jim just loud enough for only him to hear. Chloe removed her silk jacket revealing a white cotton tank top which was very plain but made of the beautiful, heavy cotton that Japanese brands occasionally use. It was thin enough to mold itself to what was underneath—the outline of her small breasts as well as the distinctive shape of clamps affixed to her nipples linked by a thin chain of metal rings. It was almost impossible not to look. It was fascinating. Unexpected. Jolting. Erotic in a completely quiet way. As if she had done all and seen all. Yet she appeared still so young. Jim could not tell how old she was, and even after, when he discussed it with Julie, he still could not wrap his head around it. She seemed ageless, with the body of a nymph and the face of a mature woman, barefoot in her big loft.

Julie looked at the device under the T-shirt and smiled. The shoot was already done for her, and she knew that Chloe had intended it to be so, that she had wanted to make it easy for them from the very first shot. Julie decided right there and then that she was not going to be directed so easily.

"I asked you to come early because of the light," Chloe said. "It moves very quickly at this time of day, and we only have a small window of time." The slanting sun lit up faint dust particles in the Soho loft where there was nothing to impede the trajectory of the light. With its glossy white walls and shiny zinc ceiling, the space became a giant box of light. Chloe was right—it made sense to shoot early there. In the center of the loft stood a large Paulin floor sofa. A Royère blue Eléphanteau armchair was perched next to it. There was no other furniture. The chair looked particularly inviting, with its high back curling ever so gracefully forward, as if asking someone to sit on it.

Like the chain between her nipples, Jim was telling himself, *asking for someone to pull on it.* Another object begging for attention.

Jim watched Chloe move towards the huge chair, and he helped her reposition it closer to the windows, setting it next to one of the ionic columns. The light now poured in even brighter as the sun made its way around one of the iconic wooden water tanks outside. This early morning light kissed everything in its wake and seemed to be hovering just below the luminous metal ceiling. Like a wave it carried within it all the memories of past sunrises, wiping off what remained of the night.

FIVE

J IM TOOK A QUICK SIP OF NEW YORK DELI COFFEE, black as
the night that had just left them. He drank it from a blue-
and-white paper cup with ancient Greek architectural de-
tails, and he smiled as he looked at the design, similar to that of
the columns around him. The ones in the loft were made of steel—
solid old steel—yet were clearly the descendants of the marble ones
from the ancient temples and, as such, also supported oneiric fantasies of transcendence. In ancient Greece, the columns had been
fluted with twenty-four little canyons running up and down each
shaft. They were deemed to have been perfect to conjure the image
of the elusive ideal woman—the quest of all architecture until now.
Though the columns in the loft lacked those flutes, the woman in
the space was still the ideal. She was the idea. The quest. Julie
had seen it all in a flash, and he saw it too now.

CHLOE WALKED TOWARDS THE VOLUPTUOUS chair with its dark blue velvet. Her plan was to sit on it and let the blue of her eyes smear themselves along the sea of pigment along the back of the chair. She would rest her arms on it, cross her legs, and let the camera capture her indolent smile and the insolent chain. The links would fascinate under the thin cotton layer. She faced the camera with the full power of her own self, her lived life, and the sweet reflection of the nascent sun on her glorious face. She had put lipstick on, making her lips a shade lighter than dark crimson, her mouth the future recipient of promises not yet made. She was ready for her shot. For the cinematographic staircase. A light among the lights, bright and vivid.

She was about to settle herself down in the chair when Julie's voice broke the silence. "Stop! Stop right there!" Chloe froze in Julie's shadow. "You want this to be special, right?" Julie's voice was lower now.

"Yes."

"Please let me do it then. Do it my way. Let me change the expected, as beautiful as the scenario you planned may be." Chloe looked at her intently, debating. "We do not have much time," Julie went on.

Chloe waited another second and then, as if aware of what was to happen, she nodded. Jim was standing by the wooden sink, one hand on the wide slab. Julie turned to him and said, "Give me your belt." Then she grabbed Chloe's chain and led her to the column.

Somehow, she remembered an episode when she was a small child and her father took her favorite doll. The long doll looked strangely like her. With a swing of his strong arms, he had repeatedly tossed the doll high in the sky. It swirled and spun, and each time her dad caught it as it fell back to Earth. "Encore?" he'd asked. Again, and again, she'd said, *"Oui!"* and the doll went up into the sky until it caught all the light it could and then came twirling back to his waiting hands.

Julie started by taking a Polaroid picture. As the image slowly revealed itself on the glossy wet paper, she kept taking more—not many, for she knew what she wanted, and luck had little to do with it. She showed Chloe how sublime her face looked on the Polaroid print, with her neck tied up to the column by the belt. The tension in the photograph was linked to the understanding that, with her hands untied, she could release herself if she wanted to. It was also understood that someone else must have tied her up to begin with. The belt's stretchable fibers allowed it to be locked in place anywhere along its length, and its deep blue color matched that of the adjacent empty chair. Chloe looked at the picture as Julie whispered in her ear, and then she let her arms reach high up above her head, grabbed the column with both hands, and leaned her head further unto the stretched belt.

Jim watched. He saw the arc of her body cast itself along the double restraints of the hard column behind her ass and the belt tightening around her throat, straining her will to leave. He saw her nipples, hard under the white fabric, and the surprising imprint of the nipple chain. She placed one foot back against the bottom of the column, and with that move, the bottom of her shorts billowed out just a little. Somehow, at that moment, the sun hid behind another building. The loft got darker, and it seemed to be the end of the shoot until, a few moments later, out of nowhere the sun hit a large window panel on a distant building and the glittering surface reflected a light so magical that the whole room was transformed again.

They all knew that this quality of light would last for just a few seconds. Julie took her time. She looked at Chloe, willing her to arch her body even more, and took three last pictures. One straight on, and the other two at 45-degree angles, left and then right, revealing in those angles the space that existed between her body and the solid metal column she was grabbing with her extended hands like a tight human bow.

The shoot was really over now, and Julie placed all of the day's films and Polaroids on the countertop. She turned around and that is when she saw, peering out of the open bedroom door, the still half-asleep face of a young woman. Chloe nodded. They left.

"Don't worry, I'll get you another belt," Julie told Jim as they reached the cobblestone streets.

SIX

T HE NEXT DAY, THE SUN WAS STILL playing hide-and-seek with only the top branches, but she was already out jogging while listening to Lee "Scratch" Perry. Nothing like reggae to get the run going when the night is still lingering in the Western clouds, she thought.

She was almost done with the five-mile loop when a text message from Jim came through. The digitized voice of her phone read out loud, *Check the last image that Chloe just sent us.* She hesitated for a step or two and then, too curious to wait, stopped. She found the picture right away. It was the very last shot she had taken, the one from the right side. In it, Chloe stood still and beautiful, wrapping herself around the column both willingly and forcefully. In the back of the loft, the door to the bedroom was open, and the head of a beautiful face could be seen looking out, an unexpected witness to it. A fantastic twist of tension. The photograph looked great, with a double narrative now: the woman tied up, and what appeared to be an innocent voyeur in the background. She started running again. Luck did have a role, she realized, and smiled. 'I deserve a little luck', she thought as she sprinted the death of her husband away.

Back home, she looked outside her window at the city that was slowly shaking itself to life while she drank her tea. Lots of windows were still dark with sleep. She'd picked up running more seriously when he left. Well, not really left. More like vanished. She took another sip from her cup, basking in that feeling of having completed her run. The tea felt great as its heat traveled down her body. They used to drink tea together. One moment drinking tea, and then gone the next. That moment gone. Forever. "Did I enjoy those moments with him enough?" she would sometimes wonder. And always get the same answer.

SEVEN

THE CITY WAS AWAKE BY THE TIME she called Jim. "She wants us back," she said.

"What do you mean?"

"Chloe wants us to go back to the loft."

"Why? More pictures of her?"

"Actually, none of her. Of her 'roommate' this time around. And she wants us to do it at sunset," she added.

"Ha!" said Jim. "When?"

"Tonight," Julie answered. "The weather switches by to-morrow. It will be a full moon—that often happens," she added. "Can you make it?"

"Well. . . ."

She could hear the hesitation in his voice—the tone of someone torn between two options and forced to decide on the spot. She had learned over time never to hesitate, to say 'yes' right away. But then again, she had a mother to thank for that. "Hesitation is a sign of faltering," her mother would say, "and the prelude to failures." From her end of the phone call she willed Jim mentally.

"Yes," he finally said, this time in a firm voice. She knew what that meant; some girl would have to wait for another day to see him.

They got there before sunset. Julie wanted to get a better feel of the bedroom, knowing that, shortly, the light would stream in for just a short while. The space that delineated the room was centered around a sunset-facing window. There were no paintings on the walls. A bed opposite the window and a chair were the only pieces of furniture in the room. Both the headboard and the chair were made of wood and Jim appreciated their craftmanship at first glance. They were honest and beautiful. The headboard was a sumptuous slab with a free edge, and wherever the wood showed signs of stress, the designer had reinforced them with elegant butterfly joints of walnut. "They're Nakashimas," Jim whispered with wonder, running his fingers over the headboard's smooth surface.

Chloe switched on her speakers, and music filled the room, moody and melancholic. Julie recognized the tracks. It was Lee Moses, with a voice full of setting suns, singing the blues like wings of birds that you want to follow with your mind. The melodies vibrated in the space as the light began to change.

With its empty white walls, being in the bedroom was like being surrounded by a thousand waves of light. Julie knew that everything could switch quickly now. She told Chloe that they might have just a few minutes of the magical "golden hour." Chloe went to the bathroom and got ready. Julie told Jim to stand by the window and take pictures at will, following his own intuition. She would stay in the main loft, shooting through the open door.

"What do you think will happen? Who's that other person?" Jim asked.

"Whatever and whoever it is just take pictures. That is all we're here to do," Julie said, and looking at him in the eyes, she added, *"Capisce?"*

"Yes. I get it." He answered as he walked into the room and settled in the corner, so that Julie would not see him in her own shots.

Chloe came out of the bathroom. She had changed into a small, translucent negligee that looked as if it was straight from the '60s. She was accompanied by a woman, who was as naked as the air and who closely followed Chloe to the bedroom.

Everything thereafter unfolded wordlessly, suggesting they had planned it ahead of time. They moved as if following an inner choreography, with the young one's motions flowing like a dancer's. The fading sun captured her body as she gracefully stood up on the bed. She had short, cropped hair, and her face was beautiful, with thick eyebrows. Her lips were wide and very red as if filled with unbound desire. Her eyes were almond-shaped and had a look of both intelligence and mischief. But it was mainly her body that breathed mischievousness, gleaming as it breathed the assurance of an inner truth. Jim continuously took pictures of her, as if making love to her image and Chloe was lying on the bed looking up at the sumptuous girl's body kissed by the golden light, as if kissed by a god. The sun shimmered along her thighs and vanished into the shadows of her void. Right then Julie took her first picture, for she was waiting like a hunter for the perfect opportunity. On the screen, she could see the thin line that hugged the girl's body, seemingly capturing even more light along its path, like the edge of a cloud — the edge of a precipice. For a brief instant she saw the light concentrate itself exquisitely along that thin layer of space, and that's when she took the shot, capturing that one instant that never ever would come back. Not for Julie. Nor for the girl with the luscious, tanned body that Chloe was now easing down toward her.

The girl's eyes lingered on Julie a second longer, as if to tease the camera, and then, with a pirouette of delight, she spread her legs open on Chloe's lips. She looked at the camera again and leaned back, all the while smiling at Julie, and with a flick of her hand she pulled up Chloe's negligee, revealing her glorious legs.

Julie had captured the initial arc of the girl as she reached back, and she knew it was good—perhaps good enough for the whole shoot. But she also knew that it would not stop there. She could feel that the young girl wanted to show off for her, for Julie. Not for Jim, who was shooting from all angles and speeds, and who kept repeating, "*Capisce! Capisce! Capisce!*" to himself in order to resist his growing temptations. No, this was all a show for Julie.

The girl's hips were flowing up and down along the raised moving tongue while she held the soft wooden edge of the headboard with one hand and opened her buttocks with the other. Julie was admiring the balanced harmony of it all. The axis of Chloe's beautiful legs pinned by the girl sitting on her face and the triangle shaped by the arm resting against the headboard. It was life over death, submission over love. She saw it all as Jim came out very quietly and whispered to her, "What next?"

"Next, we leave," said Julie as she removed the film from her camera. Jim did the same. They left the cartridges on the floor, discharging them as you would empty the shells of a shotgun, and then they silently walked out. When the girl looked around again, they were both gone.

EIGHT

TWO DAYS LATER, JULIE WAS AT HOME IN THE EVENING. She had a beautiful flat high up in the Manhattan skies, close enough to Central Park that she could run there whenever she wanted. She had surrounded herself with books and objects of beauty that she'd accumulated when Henry was still alive. Through them, he was still alive and through her, through her flesh, her eyes, he was still alive. He was alive through the fingers she would let linger, and even through the occasional man she would let linger. She was past sad now, even though the winds of hollow emptiness would sometimes sweep her off her feet, suddenly and unexpectedly, flattening her to the ground and pinning her and her sobs on the eternally grateful earth. Most of the time though, she was herself—beautiful inside, and therefore, even more beautiful on the outside.

She was reading, music playing softly in the background, when the phone rang. She put her book down, but not recognizing the number on her screen she didn't answer at first. By the third call, she did.

"Hello, Julie," a woman's voice said. It was slightly high-pitched, as if excited or anxious.

"Hello, there," Julie answered cautiously.

"My name is Victoria," the voice rushed on. "I'm Chloe's friend. The one you took pictures of a few days ago."

"Oh, yes! Good evening, Victoria. What can I do for you?" She could feel the weight of the silence on the other end of the line, as if the caller wanted to be probed some more. ". . . Yes, Victoria? Are you OK?" she asked again.

"Yes," the answer finally came. "All OK here, it's just that. . . ."

"That what?" Julie softly inquired.

"That. . .well. . .I cannot stop thinking about you filming us, taking pictures of us the other day. I absolutely loved it! I need it! I want to do it again," the voice went on, more confidently now, speaking almost in staccato.

"Well, we're flattered. Maybe we can do another session again soon," said Julie, about ready to end the conversation.

"You don't understand! I cannot wait! I want it *now*."

"My dear, it's too late now. We can schedule something with Chloe."

"I don't need Chloe for what I want to do," Victoria said firmly. "I will pay you," she added, "twice the usual amount." Julie looked outside, staring at the dark clouds beyond the top of the buildings. She let her gaze dissolve into the fabric of the distant space. The girl was so insisting, it almost felt as if she had to acquiesce just to placate her. "Alright. What do you want to do, exactly?"

In halting words, Victoria breathed out the rest of her request. She said that since she had been filmed it was all she could think about. That she wanted to do it again. That she wanted to satisfy the powerful exhibitionist impulse that kept swelling within her, like a flower wanting to open. She had waited and waited but could wait no longer. She was alone in the same loft they'd used the last time, *her* loft by the way, and that what she wanted was very specific. She wanted to pleasure herself while being recorded, and she could wait no longer. She wanted to switch to a video call and for Julie to record it all on her own camera. Or take pictures. Or whatever she thought right—not *appropriate*, for none of this was appropriate.

Julie listened to the seemingly endless flow of words and heard herself say, "Yes. OK. I will do it." She said it for the craziness of it all, and a little bit for Henry.

Shortly after, when the live image was eventually connected, Julie could see that Victoria wore red garters linked to a belt around her waist. She was sitting on a white mat with her legs open, facing a floor-to-ceiling mirror. *The bathroom*, thought Julie. The lights were dim, and she could make out the flicker of candles. She could hear music in the background and by pure coincidence, or maybe not, it was also Thievery Corporation, the same band she had just been listening to. That was an omen for her that it was indeed OK to do this and proceed with the recording. She smiled.

"I am recording you now, Victoria," she said.

Upon hearing this, the girl brought her hand to her lips and let saliva pour onto her fingers. She was wearing a black see-through blouse that parted open just enough to give a glimpse of the fullness of her breasts. One hand held the phone towards the mirror; the other had slid below. Julie could see, reflected in the mirror, the image of her small pussy opening up under the pressure of her fingers.

Julie had placed her phone on the table, against the still warm cup of tea, and was recording it all through a small separate camera, reflecting on the many intertwined digital layers that co-existed between the wonders of the initial image of the beautiful, tender flesh and the final screen of its destination. She saw on that same screen the fingers entering the girl smoothly, two digits at a time.

I'm on video? Julie heard through the speakerphone.

"Yes, dear," she answered, feeling an urge to talk to her. To coerce her. But instead, too uncomfortable with that idea, she remained a silent observer. The girl leaned over and rested her phone against the mirror, making sure that the camera scanned her body entirely. "Can you still see?" she asked, breathing harder as she took the handle of her hairbrush and slowly, slowly and deliberately, inserted it in her own pussy, letting it go in and out. Slowly at first, and then harder, and then even harder. Her back was on the floor now. Her legs opened even wider. The red lace of the garters framed the pink handle as it slid up and down, in a task never dreamed of by its Belgian manufacturer. She had two hands on it now, bringing it deeper and deeper. Her moans grew louder and seemed to merge with the reggae rhythm in the background.

"More," she whimpered. "Please tell me to do more. I beg you." She repeated that request over and over, her voice louder each time.

So Julie did. She broke her silence and said in a flat voice, "More. Do more."

Victoria went faster and Julie could see the pleasure trickling out of the girl. "*Ohhhh!*" Victoria's raspy moans came in short, deep bursts as she went even faster. Julie focused her phone on the point where all seemed to merge —the girl's torso with its curved flanks, the crack of her round ass, her legs wrapped in red silk like Christmas gifts, and, in the center of it all, her wet gleaming pussy, filled to the hilt by the hairbrush handle she was squeezing hard between her hands.

"Tell me more! Tell me to put it in my ass," asked the girl breathlessly, "Tell me, please!"

By then, Julie had decided she would leave all caution behind. "Put it in your ass" she said softly.

The girl's hand opened her buttocks and with the other, she pushed the pink handle up, coming down on it with the fervor of pain and domination. "More," she begged. "More! *Please!*"

Julie knew she could not stop there. She had become an accomplice, a partner. A paid one, but an accomplice, nonetheless. She did not have to think too much about what should happen next as she saw Victoria grab something from her left side. A dark glass bottle, cylindrical and thick appeared on Julie's screen. "I've always wanted to do this," she told Julie. "Every time I wash my hair with it." She placed the bottom end of the bottle against her open lips. It was big. Not huge, but bigger than any cockhead Julie had seen in her lifetime. The green color was perfect. A great contrast with the pink, Julie remarked to herself. *There's some beauty here,* she thought as she found herself watching yet not really seeing. "You do not need to do this," she said.

"I do. I do. I do," moaned Victoria. "For you, I want to do it. I want to." Victoria's lashes fluttered as she angled herself and pushed even harder, spreading herself open for the camera so Julie could see. And she pushed and pushed, juices pouring out of her, the bottle inching its way in her. Her whimpers had their own rhythm, expectant and pleading.

Finally, Julie said, "You can do it. Do it. Do it. *Do it.*"

Victoria did not disobey.

The moans got louder, and, in an instant, what had seemed impossible was done. The bottle with the rounded edge disappeared into her. Out of the mirror. Out of the camera screen miles away. Into an inner, tender explosion of joy at the feeling of having all her openings plugged. No way to escape herself anymore. No way not to enjoy the cascade of pleasure as the left hand brought the bottle up and down and the fingers of the right hand were leading her to a climax that seemed to defy all previous orgasms. The long fingers were moving so fast that Julie almost thought the recording was fast-forwarding itself. What she was capturing on screen was like life precipitating itself forwards and outward, or like a moon releasing a thousand waves. It submerged the bathroom in colors that Julie could not see but in which Victoria exploded into, losing herself in the plenitude of loving oneself.

Later on, Julie texted her: *Hope you're alright, dear. Put on a cold compress if needed. What do you want me to do with the film?*

She stared at Victoria's reply: *I'm fine. Ready to go to sleep now. Will have a compress as companion :) Keep the film. Was always meant for you at any rate. I paid already via the app. Thanks much.*

THE NEXT MORNING, JULIE MET JIM for breakfast. They sat at a table outside the café. There was still a touch of coolness in the air. She was hungry; her early runs did that to her. He was drinking his coffee black while she had a cappuccino. In the middle of a light conversation, she handed him an envelope. He looked at her inquisitively. "I ended up doing an extra photo shoot last night. This is your half," she said.

"Well!" he answered, not opening the envelope, "You must tell me all about it."

She sipped her coffee, a small smile on her lips, "This one will be my secret."

He nodded, understanding that silence was warranted. "But keep the money," he said as he handed the envelope back. "I did nothing to earn it."

She raised an eyebrow at him. "Yes, you did. One way or another, you did. And we are partners, so that is how it goes."

"Well, I was taking pictures, too," he said laughingly, "but I didn't get paid for it!"

"Good practice then," she said, taking a bite of her croissant.

"Precisely!" he said with a smile as he grabbed it in turn and took a bite from the other end.

NINE

THE HUSBAND WANTED HIS WIFE like smoke wants to rise: to rise, and surround, and envelope her with all his might, all his breath, and all his strength. He took her, over and over, and day, and night. And she, of the gleaming eyes, let him do so, giving herself, torrential and open and truly a gift to him in all the ways of life and love and lust. He did to her all the things men did to women. Starting with the kisses. Kisses up and kisses down. Then, with the pulsing of his manhood deep in her, he would whisper all at once words of praise and promises and requests in her ear. "Yes," was always her answer. And she meant it. She wanted to give it to him, from the top or from behind, legs spread open as he asked for and her weight shifting on his shaft with the pure delight of riding everything higher. This, and all the other things, she would do in order to hear him finally breathe with the rhythm of a forge. She allowed herself to become the clay beneath him, one that he molded to his liking. And he loved her for that and for all the beauty she brought to the pages of his life. She was the light that illuminated him, that made him shine like the early morning clouds responding to the first caresses of the rising sun.

Yet for all she did and allowed him to do, she did not let him strap her neck, nor did she allow more than a probing finger or slender toy within the confines of her tacit opening. He did not personally need it to happen, for he was in constant bliss, but somehow, he felt the need for it to be done. He wanted to witness her total abandon, and to have her float to the other side of that swollen river. He wanted it without knowing why. He had an inner desire whose origins he could not quite elucidate, and he had long ceased to try to understand it all.

She, the wife, with beautiful hair and dark eyes, could also not quite understand the attraction she felt, now and then, for men who were not him—for those not her beloved husband. Like this morning at the gym, when a young man had looked at her with eyes that told her all. Surprisingly, she had liked that look and the way his eyes had traveled over her body molded by the stretched fabric of her workout attire. She had liked it enough to arch her spine just a little more, sloping her butt back and pushing her breasts forward in the most shameful way. She had eventually cut the elliptical routine short and left the gym before things could progress, aware of the scoping eyes.

TEN

Julie and Jim did eventually get busy. Through word of mouth, they got calls, from vibrant singles to adventurous couples, ready to become more than shadows as their outlines got recorded on film.

There was the golden girl with curls that laced her face and naked shoulders like a shower of lust, whose hair barely covered her nipples as Jim took aim at her, hands shaking despite himself, repeating the *"Capisce"* mantra to keep his desire within the confines of the hard box camera, especially when she, mischievous as she was, flicked her head back and revealed her berry skin and its promises of not-so-hidden pleasure. Yet he stayed the course. Julie looked at him with a smile, taking over the shoot as the girl laid her frame forward across a large gray exercise ball and flaunted, for all to see, her perfect spherical butt strapped tightly by a dark thong. Her foot curled up strategically and hid the focus of all gazes. It was the hidden that enthralled more than the exposed. The guess of more, of must discover. This was especially true for men who viewed these images. It was also a fact uncannily understood by women who laid themselves bare. The girl lying down on the exercise ball was not shy. She wanted a *picture* taken. She was not trying to seduce Jim. She wanted to seduce a wider audience, away from touch and consequence. As the shoot went on, she was revealing more and more, and each image was a word in a story she unveiled about herself.

Julie always took the best images. Or almost always. Jim had to admit it. He tried hard, even imitating her, and yet he seemed to fall short. His pictures were great, definitely "Instagrammable," but hers were magical. It was as if her camera alone could capture the narrative of hidden emotions, the potential of incarnation. The Native Americans allegedly refused to have their pictures taken, declaring that it would rob them of their souls, as if the soul would get sucked up into the images. But now, in a fashion quite dramatically the reverse of that belief, people seem to build their souls by taking more and more pictures. Adding layer and layer of photographs, each another brick in the illusion of a house they build around themselves.

ELEVEN

THE COUPLE, THE ONE WITH THE WIFE whose beauty attracted the eyes and the loving husband who could not take all of her, had contacted Julie to set up a photo shoot. They wanted it as soon as possible. That night even, if possible. By then, Julie knew that evening shoots did carry added weight. Like a tacit understanding that, by coming after the sun went down, one entered a world closer to mysteries and tempting darkness.

She was OK with an evening shoot. She appreciated how it could create tension that was good for the photos and the liquid representation of reality. Besides, she liked the nights. Henry had always been fond of them. Sometimes, she still met him in the night. Back when he was alive, it was easy and natural. At times, in the middle of the night, his strong body would curl upon her and find her. The months of him being gone hadn't made him disappear. There were times, even with a clear mind, when she would sense his scent again, and then her legs would get warm like they used to. And she would then see his image again and would whisper to him, "Come, you can take me. I'm still yours." And if there happened to be a young body in bed next to her, she would let him fulfill her.

She and Jim arrived that same evening at the couple's house. It was a townhouse, very elegant, a carriage house in a past era housing horses for the Fifth Avenue mansions. Now it was furnished with manicured class and taste. Julie noticed beautiful pieces of Art Nouveau furniture, the lacquered wood picking up the light of chandeliers. 'A good backdrop for a photo shoot,' she thought. These pieces, expensive when they were first made were now so priceless that no one could afford to either sell them or buy them. So, they remained like faithful servants in their owners' houses, glittering away the souls of their makers and reflecting the days floating by.

The husband, a voluble chap, obviously nervous, moved his narrow frame from room to room, asking Julie, "Where do you want to take us?"

You mean, *take our picture*, Julie thought. But she let it slide, for she knew that the pictures were much more than images, especially when two people were to be photographed. For one thing, how could both of them look at their best at the same time? It was like having two lights flashing independently and hoping for them to flash simultaneously, only to separate again.

He brought them to the bedroom. There, his speech got even faster. He spoke about everything and nothing. He was so excited to have them enter the wide room with the king-sized bed and, almost as expected, a late De Kooning oil facing the bed. It was a painting that immortalized on canvas the few and final strokes of a mind that only had a few strokes left.

Julie was still not sure what this fast-talking, babbling, nervous man was all about. She could hear in the adjacent bathroom the ding and cling of glass jars being moved on what was most likely a white marble countertop. She turned back on her heels and walked away from the bedroom and its huge bedspread, the opalescent gray surface floating like an ice rink of taffeta in the middle of the house. She left the iciness and walked back to the living room, where the objects made of warm wood spoke to her and her sensibilities. The husband remained silent until he saw her set up the camera and tripod. "Oh, here," he said, slightly dejected.

"Yes, here," she said, and he retreated in the direction of the bedroom and its two adjoining bathrooms.

Jim had been following them around all this time and had not said a word. It was all new to him, the opulence, the thing they called "decorated" in which an architect and an interior designer regulated the rhythm of lives. To someone like Jim, who shared a room and a small bathroom with countless siblings, it was alien. He felt out of his element yet not too surprised by it all. The house did fit the square grid of the city, where all of nature was condensed to fit into Central Park. And then, the wife walked into the room. Jim took one look at her and was faced with the revelation of nature's beauty all over again. He had expected a tall blonde girl with high cheekbones. But no, this one was unusual—dark in complexion, as if permanently tanned, and of such varied ethnicity that neither he nor Julie could identify her origins. She was like one of those spoils of war from a distant past that had been captured and recaptured, and through the passing of centuries and dilution of bloodlines, had never been able to assimilate again to any race or country. Regardless of where she came from, she was superb. Jim looked at the husband with a silent smile. "Much respect," he said to himself.

Julie was not surprised, for she had expected nothing. She knew better. She had half expected that the wife would be wearing some ornate affair, like a gown, with some sparkle or weird shapes, but she was pleasantly surprised by the simple outfit. The wife was simply in a white T-shirt that covered her small breasts and wore with it a pleated, mid-thigh navy blue skirt. There were no high heels. No shoes at all, actually. The glitter of the stone on her left hand was the sole sparkle. Well, that and her eyes, which were gleaming brighter against her own will when she saw Jim.

She was not very tall, but with her posture, the way she

kept her shoulders back, and the thick black hair crowning her head, she still filled the room, like a small painting on a museum wall that somehow steals the show despite having much larger ones around it. She was just like that, her beauty contained within yet visible on each surface of her being. And then revealed even more when she nonchalantly removed her T-shirt before a word was said.

Her eyes stared straight into Jim's, and he found it difficult to retain his detachment, whipped as he was by that visual lash. Her eyes were aglow as she looked at him—dark eyes that shone like obscure stones, like two parallel beams of desire. That stare could have burned through falling snow, leaving the snowflakes falling in a radiant cascade of silent bystanders. That is what they had all become, silent bystanders in a trance, enamored by her being.

They were there to shoot people in various states of undress, varying degrees of nudity, and everything was expected. But never had someone so bluntly revealed her body and intentions. Even Julie, who had seen it all, stopped and stared. There seemed to be no one else in the old carriage house. No maid, no dog, no kids. Presumably, all had been sent ahead to the weekend house. Maybe that's why the husband had wanted it so badly to happen tonight. And happen it would, for the stage had already been set and the play written.

The husband came closer to her, and, with infinite sweetness and kind tact, she avoided his touch and had him sit on a solitary Dunand armchair. The light blue silk that covered the chair engulfed as much as excluded him. Meanwhile exotic dance rhythms surrounded them now, the music adding yet another layer of surreal atmosphere to the whole experience.

Jim looked at the husband straight in the eyes, neither inquisitive nor judgmental. He was just looking, almost curious. And he got the sign. The signal. The slight nod of the head, and then another nod towards the disrobed, mythical creature who was his wife.

Julie saw it all, and when Jim turned towards her, this time with a quizzical look, she answered with a smile, and he took that as a seal of approval. The dice had rolled a little further.

He approached the wife, camera in hand. She moved to the end of the living room and sat on a wide, chocolate-colored sofa framed in bright bronze. It was floating in the back of the large living room, making it appear as if she was resting on her own island. The only light in that corner was coming from a beautiful Tiffany lamp with a glass shade of dripping wisteria. It was in the dimness that he found her.

She recalled the words her husband had spoken moments earlier in the hallway: "Just do it already. Do it for me."

And as soon as she heard the words again in her mind, she dismissed them, for she wanted no one, nothing, to enter her mind just then. She wanted to be *there*, on the sofa, eyes halfclosed in the dim light as if falling ever further away from reality.

And in that moment, she found Jim's hips and undid his belt. It slipped out noiselessly as she pulled on it, and it rested in her hands at first, and then around her slender neck as she placed it there, the end of the strap slipping back into the metal loop of the silver buckle. And then, as she finished unbuttoning him, and still being recorded, she slipped his swelling cock into the warmth of her hungry young mouth.

The husband looked up and saw that Julie was recording it all. He was swept into a cloud by what he was watching. It was everything he had always expected but never thought could happen. There was a small red light on the camera indicating a video being recorded between pictures being taken. It was stunning to realize that the heat of what was happening right there, on the fateful sofa, was also being frozen in time in Julie's camera.

Both husband and camerawoman knew what would follow. Julie moved further to the side, and she took a full view of the couple on the sofa. And then switching to a wider-angle mode, she encompassed in the same frame the wife, whose mouth was linked to Jim's midsection and whose skirt had been hoisted, revealing all of her, as well as the husband, looking at it all from the confines of the luxurious chair that sealed his non-participation. That would be the shot of the evening, she thought. The one with all the tension that such a moment demanded. And the one she might want to keep aside, she reflected, as she toyed with the idea of storing it in the hard drive of the camera.

Jim experienced the woman with the excitement one gets from a rare, ultimate surprise. He found himself loving her in that moment, and his manhood rose at the idea of the gift she was offering him—he let himself slip into her mouth with the abundance of a river full of lust. Somehow his thoughts wandered. She reminded him of that tree he was asked to take down long ago, when his dad had told him to cut a few of them for winter wood. For a moment, he was back home, in his youth, in the days of wielding sharp axes. Back then, he had kept the biggest tree of the lot for last. He remembered the long crack that ran along the trunk of it, going from the onset of the first branch down to the earthy roots—like an opening for fairy tales and future elves, a crack of such strength and beauty within the dark wood that he had run his fingers along its edge before slamming the axe. With his fingers now, he followed the line of her naked spine and the beginning of her ass as he stripped her of her skirt and started pulling on the belt. His fingers found the pure line of her pleasure, a meridian that ran from the base of her skull down to the apex of her ass and beyond to where fluids gathered in a fountain of anticipation. And with fingers wet with her own juices, he opened her, opened the forbidden. The belt around her neck rested lazily in his hand as her hips danced languidly with him, a clear indication of her acquiescence.

That is when, with a look of understanding to Julie who was filming it all, the husband left the room. . .content that he could, and would, review it all later, when she left the films for him in exchange for the envelope filled with cash by the entrance door. Even as he stepped away, he could see Jim, belt in hand, beginning to ride his wife.

The wife was focused on the pure pleasure he was giving her, and her body melted for him under asphyxia, pain, and orgasm all at once. The outline of her slender shape reflected divinely onto the polished doors of the sumptuous ebony Ruhlmann cabinet, a real-life fresco made to last the longest of instants. Her neck was up high and deliberately tight against the leather strap, her pelvis rising up and down along his engorged shaft that eventually released itself within the confines of her deepest being.

That was when Julie stopped recording. The real event, as well as the one reflected in the furniture.

She moved to the girl, released the belt, gave it back to Jim, and slipped the T-shirt back on the woman. She stroked her hair as she laid her down on the sofa and under a nearby cashmere blanket. The wife snuggled against the softness of the chocolate wool of the sofa, giving herself up to Julie's touch, with eyes closed, and a quiet smile on her lips.

Before anyone could really think about anything, Julie and Jim were gone. The films were where the envelope had been, and together in a taxi they headed downtown for at least one celebratory drink after realizing that they had been very generously overpaid.

TWELVE

SEX WITHOUT HENRY WAS LIKE picking orgasms out of thin air. As if she was walking down a row of apple trees with someone and suddenly, pushed by hunger and the sight of a beautiful fruit, she would pick it and bring it to her mouth, her hand pushing that fruit deep in, letting all the juices deliver themselves within her, tasting the sweetness that cracked straight out of the flesh and onto her lips and tongue. She did not care which person walked with her along the apple grove or from which limb or tree the fruit came. She just picked it up and brought it to her mouth. Naked in skin and in expectations. Living it now because later will not happen, not anymore.

Towards the end, she enjoyed drinking tea with Henry when that was still possible. She did it from the deepest confines of her soul. Each sip of the hot liquid connecting her ever closer to his soul, his being, as they sat in silence, letting the warmth descend on them, just like the spoonful of honey melting in the elegant wooden cups. She had found the two cups in a small Japanese store in a half-hidden courtyard in the Quartier Latin in Paris, that store now long gone. She had one cup left for herself while the other one rotted away in the earth beside him, where it belonged.

THIRTEEN

THEIR NEXT CLIENT WAS A MAN FROM PARIS named Alexander. In his mid-thirties, he had resolved to follow his father's advice to settle down and raise a family. He had lived the wild life of youth, and he knew that he was ready. For some time, he had been seeing the color of his existence shift away as the seasons passed.

In the Big Apple, he was dating three different women. They were wonderful. Really wonderful. All three of them. He just could not make up his mind. He felt he had to get closer to them, to know their inner identity. He had to observe them from up close and afar all at once, and he had to see them naked. Or almost naked, for he had not touched any of them yet and wished not to do so until he was ready.

The client took a cue from ancient mythology when he decided to pick one of them. It is said that when Paris, a mortal, was asked to assess who among the three goddesses, Athena, Hera, and Aphrodite, was the most beautiful, he asked them to disrobe in order to better judge them.

The women all agreed to have their pictures taken by Julie and Jim, since they truly wanted to impress him. He was handsome and hard-working, and rich in both money and manners: a good boy who would surely become a great man to one of them and a responsible father to their children. So, they let J&J come to their homes and disrobed for him through their lenses.

The first was wonderfully strong and muscular. She worked out with weights, sometimes with men. She ran a lot, and the tension of her muscles was visible under the surface of her soft skin, yet she kept a feminine shape with wide hips that would deliver children easily, and breasts that could soon fill with fat and milk. Her name was Anna. "The Anna," she sometimes referred to herself, unaware that she was a distant descendant of Athena.

For the shoot, in her one-bedroom apartment high up in the corner of a tall East Side building, she chose an early afternoon appointment. The light streamed in bright and flat through the untreated window, casting deep shadows. As Julie and Jim set up, she stretched her long body toward the sun as if she were about to begin an event, a race. In his mind Jim traced a line that ran from her small finger up along the side of her arm and then down to her waist. She was already naked except for the cotton thong that fantastically enhanced her strong cheeks. He smiled at her fabulous derriere. "What a dream job I have," he told himself for the nth time.

She had on little make-up, but her thick hair had been professionally done. The blonde mane rested like a gleaming helmet on her skull. She could choose the shoot, they'd told her, and style it as she wished.

At the last minute she chose to sit down on the table, wrapping her legs with her arms, offering her profile to the camera, the dark shadow on the empty wall behind her like a flagrant echo emanating straight from her. By coincidence, or perhaps not, the window's shadow appeared like a tall spear to her side. Jim was the one taking the pictures that day while Julie looked on. She tried to remain impartial, but Anna had taken one look at her and knew through Julie's eyes that the shot was not right. Anna was like an artist who steals the gaze of visitors and, through those very eyes, rediscovers the painting that otherwise seems to disappear. Realizing that it was not her best angle, she uncurled her body, faced the window and the light, and sat on the side of the table. Her legs were seductively open and with hands flat on the surface of the table she pushed her chest forward as she smiled beyond the camera. And in doing so also beyond this picture and into a future that could depend on something as thin as an alignment of pixels in the net of destiny.

Back home, Julie looked at the shots. The girl was a war-rior regardless of her pose. She picked the softest one on be-half of Anna and gently softened it some more, smoothing the sharp edges of the brilliant sunlight.

The second woman's name was Haley. Since her middle initial was "E" and her last name started with an "R," she sometimes referred to herself simply as "Her." Everything about 'Her' was present and solid. She had the presence of a young diva who could fill any room with the thunder of her being. She wanted Alexander for she believed he might yield the lightning that she knew should precede her.

She entered the room that Julie and Jim had set up wea-ring a long, translucent, black silk gown revealing beneath it the lattice of dark purple lace that crisscrossed her breasts and thighs. She wanted Alexander to be transported by her looks. She was tall, firm, and moved like royalty. Slowly. Delib-erately. With an emphasis on each step. When Jim looked at her, mesmerized, she knew it was good. It was evening and they were all in her bedroom. The proximity of them all, the dimmed light, and the nudity made it feel very intimate. Both Julie and Jim took turns taking pictures of her lying on her bed with her hair sprawled to her side, and the folds of the see-through gown scattered around her like delicate petals of a dark flower that bloomed only at night.

She insisted on selecting the final shot. In it, her eyes were looking deep into the viewer's, and her hand settled between her legs, fingers interlocked into the black fabric, her crimson nails a token of her mind. Shot from above, it was a sight to behold—an invitation to a river of no return. Julie agreed it was the best shot for her.

The third woman to be photographed for Alexander from Paris was named Angelica. Once again, it was an evening shoot, though this time a little earlier. The sun was just setting, leaving behind it a trace of light. Only the planet Venus could be seen in that special dark blue hue seen only in the New York City sky at dusk. She was playing Eric Satie on the sound system when they walked in, and she greeted them fully clothed, in tight black leather pants and a lightweight black cashmere sweater. Jim thought he could make out the shape of her breast under the luxurious fabric, but she moved all the time, and he could not rest his gaze long enough to really appreciate its full impact. He stopped trying and instead took in her entire presence. She moved with delight, each step a note of joy. She did not offer them tea but instead brought Irish whiskey in short glasses without ice and pretzels. Jim wanted that salt. He licked his lips and let the drink burn. They were both waiting for her to get ready, but she did not seem to make a move. And so, after a little while and with her empty glass in hand, Julie asked, "Do you want to change at all before the shoot?"

"No need," answered Angelica. "I am ready now."

"When do you want to start?" asked Julie.

Looking outside she answered, "Now is good" and then

moved closer to the window and sat on a chair by a small '50s vintage desk. In the far distance a cloud drifted, and suddenly light poured in, illuminating her sensuous body though it still remained clad in her black outfit. She was the ultimate city girl, confident and unassuming.

Jim took a first shot, the noise of the shutter resonating in sync with the piano concerto. He took another shot as she reached her arms up slowly, uncrossing them and taking the whole sweater off in one fell swoop. Through his lens he now saw them, glorious and big and heavy with the weight of future desires. Whatever light was left in the sky seemed to follow her.

Julie started shooting, too. There was no time to stage the scene, yet the girl was a natural. The camera loved her. Her dark hair flowed along the side of her thin pale face. Her eyes were shaped as if created generations earlier. The music filled the whole room as the remaining sunlight disappeared. She inched forward and sat at the edge of the chair, at the very edge, resting her weight upon the toes of her black patent leather shoes and slowly, deliberately, opened her legs for both of them to see, peering through the cut-out shape of her pants' crotch, the beauty of her naked rose, a flash of pink matched only by the veneer of her nails. She laid her hands on her thighs and smiled. She smiled at the camera, at Alexander, at Paris. At the Paris that was waiting. Always waiting for such a thing to happen. Her Mount of Venus, the fulcrum of the image, engulfed within it Jim and Julie, and any other viewer thereafter. Within her confines. Her boundaries. Her expanse. Her explosion of love.

In the end, in the Greek story, Paris, son of Priam, Alexandros by name, picked Aphrodite as the most beautiful one of the three goddesses. In return, Aphrodite gave him as a gift the most beautiful woman on Earth, Helen, wife of Menelaus. That is what started the battle of Troy, the Trojan War.

Here, Alexander, from the city of Paris, picked Angelica. It was not an easy choice, but it was a natural one. The camera had picked her. The camera never lies.

FOURTEEN

J IM HAD TO TELL SOMEONE. He occasionally talked to people about his new job, because that could potentially drum up business. But now, he felt he really had to tell someone about his belt around the neck of the wife and his manhood deep in her and how Julie had shot it all.

He had to tell a friend. He still had a few. They were the ones he knew from way back when he was a child, from home. Early friends may turn out to be disappointing, but they are the truest of friends. They'd been children when they first met and nothing had gotten in the way of them recognizing themselves to be from a common flame, a common place. Arthur was one of them. The friends he made nowadays were great, and fun, but he doubted he ever wanted to get lost in a forest with them. He had gotten lost in the forest with Arthur once.

It was a thick forest of dense pine trees up in the hills. As evening approached, the light became fainter and fainter. It was beautiful and unreal and frightening all at the same time. They were like two lost swimmers in a green ocean of sweetly scented moving branches, engulfed in the purity of nature. The air became heavy. There were no more trails, no more *direction*, only a thick, soft, uniform carpet of pine needles on the ground. Jim had climbed high up in a tree. He'd seen in the distance the lights of a farm.

That glow, he remembered, was like the welcoming smile of the wife in the townhouse.

He told Arthur about the house first, for Arthur, even though he had a fabulous name, knew little of such things. He described the rooms—the bed as big as an iced pond, the shadows of light on the veneered wood. And then he told him about the woman, omitting entirely the husband. He described her body like men do, and led Arthur through the sequence of events.

And Arthur said, "You let that other woman take pictures of you?" He was not surprised at what Jim was doing to the wife, that was par for the course, but the camera, that was unusual and strange.

"Yes," said Jim, "and the strange thing is, it felt OK." What he really wanted to say was that it had been *exciting* to have been watched.

He hung up and thought about it some more. He had also

been watched by the husband. That was not too exciting. But when Julie, eye still on the camera, had raised her thumb, he had loved it. Like a rodeo rider. And he had strangely wanted to make her proud of him. He could not talk about *that*, not even to Arthur.

He twirled the bourbon at the bottom of the tumbler, looking at the small ripples of the amber liquid in the heavy glass until he got lost in it and saw it all once again—the woman he held with the belt, tight and glistening as she opened herself up for him, and Julie looking through the lens. With a twirl of his wrist, he imagined Julie moving closer to him, leaving the camera on the tripod. In his mind's eye he saw her walking towards him, making a slight detour so as not to obscure the camera's field of view. He saw her settle behind him.

And then his phone rang.

FIFTEEN

I T WAS ARTHUR AGAIN. He wanted to know how come
Jim had not gotten the other woman involved, the one
taking the pictures. Why did he not pleasure both of them
that evening? Jim let the phone rest on his ear for a moment
and then answered, "Soon, I will let you know when it
happens" and, as he hung up, he whispered to himself "I really
hope so."

The girls were plentiful in New York, and he navigated the
city as he would a forest; taking measured steps to get to the
top of its mythical buildings, eagerly looking for home. Here
he could pretty much pick any single young girl he wanted, yet
he found himself daydreaming about Julie all the time. Each
and every time he would let his mind wander all he could see
was her radiant face. He would watch her hands as they got

closer and closer to her camera, and in his dream it was *his* body she was touching. Eyes half closed, he saw himself lying on her bed with his shirt open, waiting for her and the imagined nakedness of her curves, the shadow of her strong running legs, the flatness of her tanned belly, the smoothness of her skin. She would take his drink from his hand, take a long sip from it and, leaning forward, tenderly spill some in his expecting mouth. The tumbler was resting on his lips when his phone rang again.

This time it was her.

"Yes, Julie?" he said as he sat to attention on the side of his bed, his dark blue shirt open like the curtains of an awaiting stage. His eyes focused far away, imagining her from a distance.

"Yes," he answered when she asked if he was home, and "Yes" again when he agreed to meet her for a quick drink in fifteen minutes at a bar around the corner. He hung up, elated at the idea of seeing her so soon. In one swig he drained the remainder of his bourbon—that last sip feeling so purposeful, so complete.

HE WAS WALKING TOWARDS FANELLI'S, the local bar, thinking of the conversation he had just had with her. All he had been able to say was "Yes" three times in a row. Not his most stellar performance. She did that to him. What is she doing downtown at this hour? he wondered. Looking up, he noticed the moon framed between two Soho buildings. "Is it really full?" he murmured. He was not sure; maybe there was a missing sliver in the top right corner, a faint shadow that failed to complete the perfect disk.

Just as if he had skipped that last sip of bourbon at the bottom of the glass, as if one more breath was missing.

Inside Fanelli's, they sat side by side at the worn wooden bar. She had been waiting for him, saving his seat amid the crowd. Not an easy task, but she commanded a presence that made people think twice before they became upset. Add to it a lovely smile that illuminated her face, and people usually listened to her.

She was relieved, though, to see him finally arrive. The bar stool made a soft noise as he pushed it back to accommodate his frame. She watched him settle in his seat, looking at his built body fill the empty space beside her. They had not worked together for a few days, and seeing him again, feeling his presence, she realized how much she had missed him. Shielding her gaze, she looked ahead, smiling when she saw his reflection in the mirror. How funny is it, she thought, that we're always reflected like that, sitting side by side and facing a mirror. The image makers have their own image captured!

She had already ordered his beer. It came in a tall glass, and he took a long sip. There was almost no foam left on its surface by the time he arrived, yet it left a faint white imprint on his upper lip as he put the glass down. She smiled when she noticed it and, without even thinking, used the soft part of her right thumb to wipe his lip clean. He loved that. He wanted to take her thumb and place it in his mouth, his hands around hers. And she wanted to put it back in her own mouth, like babies do. They did nothing of the sort. Instead, she discreetly dried the thumb against the side of her jeans while Eric Clapton's song streamed in the background.

Fanelli's was where artists used to meet decades ago, when people still talked face to face and exchanged ideas. Boxers came there, too. Sometimes the artists even became boxers.

The bar is located on Mercer Street, one of the last ones in the city to be lined with those heavy gray cobblestones polished by decades of passing cars and footsteps.

"Do you know why there are cobblestones in the streets of Soho?" she finally asked Jim, breaking their shared silence.

"No."

"When British ships did commerce with these colonies many decades ago, they would leave here filled with local goods such as furs, and minerals, and other kinds of heavy stuff. But on their return voyage from England, they needed ballast, so they filled their holds with cobblestones. Once they reached the harbor here, the ballast was unloaded and roads built with it. That's why the cobblestones streets are all downtown—close to the old harbor."

He was taken by the story. "Think about how many hands each stone had to go through before landing in the street here," he said. "British stones on U.S. soil. One day for sure they'll be replaced. Everything gets replaced in the U.S. You'll see—they'll run a ribbon of asphalt along the street, and that asphalt will crack and tear in the northeastern weather. Then old people will bemoan the cobblestones that self-adjusted to the cold and heat and humidity."

She shifted on the stool. "I asked you to meet me tonight because we have to make a few decisions. And I want to do them in your presence."

"OK. Shoot." His face flushed. He wasn't quite sure where this was going. He did not want her breaking up the team. He really liked the gig. He enjoyed the work. And he loved working next to her. Already in his mind, he was planning a response.

"We have two customers who want us to come back for more shoots."

"Well, that's good news," he said, and with a sigh of relief he took one more swig of his beer.

He looked older than his age, and she looked younger. Any other bartender would have assumed they were the same age, but the guy behind the bar that night was no newcomer, and he could guess from the shape of her hand on the glass, and the speed at which he drank, that she was the mature one and he was the loving one. One glance was usually all it took him to assess someone. But with her, with the beautiful eyes and smiling face, it took more time. As if she belonged to a different layer. One he had noticed before.

Occasionally strangers wandered in, sat at the bar, and quietly filled the space around them with their mere presence. These people were rare. And he was convinced Julie was one of them. He could recognize these souls, though he never considered himself one of them. But maybe he was. It was a strange thing: others could recognize, but the individuals themselves could not. They waited to be tapped as gurus, teachers, masters, though most often they went to the other side without leaving a tangible trace. Or maybe they would leave a faint line, like the duck in the water in Central Park. Or imagine the dry space under a pine tree after a light snowfall, the dusting of snow still quivering in the branches while, under the tree's cover, around the trunk, there remains a dry green circle where you can sit safely on dry ground. Such is the imprint these particular souls create—a circle of comfort and beauty in the midst of chaos.

The bartender saw all of this in her. He kept his gaze on her a little longer and then went about serving his next customer.

"Yes," she said, "the two clients want us back, but it seems a bit different from our prior engagements. So, I have to run it by you. The first one is that woman Angelica. You remember her? The customized cut-out leather pants?"

"Of course."

"Well, she wants us to do a whole series of photographs

of her. Follow her to different locations at different times of day and night."

"I thought that Alexander, the guy from Paris, had chosen her."

"He did, but apparently, she declined his offer and instead sent her girlfriend Helena to meet him. And now those two allegedly are an item. What she wants is to have a whole portfolio of seductive photographs. She's not sure why exactly. She even spoke of maybe making a book. The issue is that we may have to be available at short notice."

"Then tell her," he suggested, "that we want to be on a retainer. With our regular fees on top when we shoot."

"I like that," she said, "but that means we'll have to be ready at the spur of the moment."

"I'm OK with it. Just make it worth our while. What's the second request?"

"Hm." She reached for her drink and took a long slow drag from the glass. "The other one is a bit trickier, and it really depends on you. Let me just say that I'm OK with any decision you make. It truly is your call."

"Shoot."

"Well, the couple from the carriage house, the one with all that fancy furniture. They'd like us to come back." She let that last sentence trail softly, as if the words were landing in a large vat of dark water.

"OK." Jim did not flinch. He did not even take a sip from

the glass the bartender had refreshed without a word. "Of course, but on two conditions. First, obviously, you should be there. And second, we go back downtown and celebrate in style right after."

And that was it, two new adventures on the horizon, a thick beer-foam mustache on his laughing upper lip, and Julie laughing with him in the dimly lit bar. Her head going back, her white teeth like pearls in her tanned face, her pink tongue partly visible between her lips, red with life, her skin glowing with joy, and the onset of her neck, fragile and slender. And then, his hand behind her neck, and for an instant, his lips on hers, just like that. Just as if it was part of the laugh. Sharing the laughter, and the lips, and the beer mustache.

She let it happen because it was spontaneous, and of the moment, and it had lasted all of a few seconds. Looking at them, the bartender smiled as he was drying a glass with a mechanical gesture repeated a thousand times and never to be improved on.

And she smiled after the kiss, as if it had been the thousandth one as well. She kept it light and airy, like a woman who knew how to react to a surprise, who knew how to honor a moment.

And a little later, as she walked back home alone, looking at the moon, she admitted to herself that she had enjoyed it. Strangely, she had enjoyed it, even though she knew there was nothing serious about it. But she could not deny it, there had been some weight behind this kiss. Behind the lips, like a breeze of ocean air that suddenly blew her hair away. "That was when I had long hair," she murmured quietly. She was too old for him now, but she could think and wink about it. "Life goes on," she had to remind herself once in a while. She should enjoy it. Whatever was left. Whatever was right.

She was glad that Jim had accepted the two assignments. Taking pictures of strangers was fun because they were strangers. New bodies, new eyes, new smiles were a gift, but it happened too fast. No time for her to understand them, really. To squeeze more out of them into her camera. To predict the shadows and the optional light. But now she would get to shoot the same people over, and in the case of Angelica, perhaps over and over. She was looking forward to that, regardless of where it brought her. . .or maybe because of it.

SIXTEEN

J IM STAYED AT THE BAR. He was so excited about his spontaneous gesture, his kiss, that he needed to stay put for a while longer. Besides, the goodbye on the street would have been awkward.

He nursed another beer for a while, and when he looked up at the bartender, he saw him pouring a shot of bourbon in a small, thick glass. "On the house," said the bartender. The drink was so full it almost spilled over. Honey-colored, it caught the light of the room—a spot of brightness on the dark, weathered surface of the bar.

"Thanks," said Jim, not even asking why. Why would he get a celebratory drink? And why did the bartender know that bourbon was his drink of choice? And how did the drink not even spill a drop? Not a drop! Slowly he bent his head, placed his lips along the rim of the glass, and raising it, emptied it in one swig. "Wow!" he said, "that hits the spot. Thanks!" With that, he paid and went home, the moon flirting with him as she appeared and disappeared—an icon of unknown substance floating between clouds and rooftops, a presence as fleeting as what the future seemed to hold.

Later on, the moonlight reached Julie's bedroom as well. It revealed itself through the frame of her window as a sharp line that cut her bed in two. The bright light spread up to the edge of her hips while her torso remained obscured in shadows. She looked at her body as if it were divided by the light. The lower part was bathed in lunar luminance, and her breasts, shoulders, and neck remained in darkness, as if in a realm of separate senses: a dichotomy she noticed in others but rarely in herself, although these instances were becoming more frequent recently. . .as if being alone had split her in two.

SEVENTEEN

NGELICA LIVED IN THE CARLYLE HOTEL. She had
moved in when a friend left the fully furnished suite
for her. She was attracted to it for two reasons: first,
because it seemed temporary, which fit her nomadic lifestyle;
and second, because of the '60s furniture that came with the
flat, which fit her current sense of style. The rent was not in-
expensive, but considering all the benefits that came with living
full-time in a five-star hotel, it was acceptable by Manhattan
standards. At any rate, money never seemed to be a huge
problem for Angelica. Either it was there, or she made it
happen.

She was beautiful, as Alexander had attested to when he
chose her, and she was naturally seductive, as some women
are, almost unwillingly so. But it was her attitude that was the

most attractive. She accepted pleasure and offered nothing to confrontation. She loved everything—the rain, the beach, the sun, the mountains. She loved her breasts when she saw them in the mirror and the swing of her hair when she moved fast. She also loved being photographed by Julie and Jim. It had felt liberating in the most natural way—like being a movie star without all the fuss. And the camera loved her back. You just could not take a bad shot of her. Face on, profile, head down. Dressed, undressed. In every shot, she was radiant.

And now, once again, in the backroom of the suite, sprawled out on a white, curved sofa, she offered her nudity to their cameras, thrilled to give up her image. She felt at ease with them. Ready to please.

That night, the room was painted in red light. Red bulbs were glowing in the floor-to-ceiling Panton chandelier made of twisted strips of silver plastic that moved in unison with the slightest motion. As the strips moved, a whisper floated, and a flood of fluctuating light bathed her naked skin.

She was wearing a long, see-through dress, black with white polka dots, tight around her tender body and widely open on her shoulders and breasts. It molded her shape, revealing all of its consequences, but hid it as well under a veil of apparent humility.

She stood at the point of inflection where the waves of both the red light and the bluish glow of the city met, like brilliant rivers cascading along her body, shading her with loving strokes. She radiated of desire as she lounged on the sofa, facing them with a broad smile, undivided in her attention and exaltation.

Long ago, ancient gods and goddesses had vanished into the firmament, leaving behind them tangible traces of their previous appearances. They left temples solid enough to withstand the test of time, and lyrical poems, and ancient devotional objects reflecting past sacrifices. And they left an essence of their being, an aura floating in thin air, there for future souls to perhaps discover and embrace. Some would become avatars of prior greatness, actors of past strength.

Angelica's had merged with the residual presence of Aphrodite. And as such, she lay on the sofa as if the city and the world wanted her to. As if many were looking simultaneously through the magical lenses of the cameras and were all gazing at her luscious body just as she slowly brought the fabric of her dress further and further up her naked legs. The ambient light, replacing the dress as she unveiled, was revealing the splendors of her flesh, reaching the tops of her thighs. She wore a very small, leopard-print silk thong that covered her like a gift. It contained absolutely everything within—from lust to conception to birth; all covered neatly in that small, stretched fabric.

Julie nudged Jim forward, guiding him to within a few feet of Angelica, whose eyes were now closed. With her head resting backward, she lifted the dress further up until her thighs were fully exposed to the camera. And Jim, like a fervent accomplice, recorded her running her fingers over the surface of the thong, finding the outline of the supreme chalice of all sacrifices.

Julie had moved to the side, and she took the shot she had been waiting for—it was of Jim with his body and camera leaning forward toward the "offering." Julie always wanted to take at least one shot at each assignment that gave her the satisfaction of having perhaps achieved some form of art. One shot for her own sake before she got back to the task of pleasing the customer.

Jim was taking that picture of Angelica, eyes still closed, fingers moving at their own rhythm along the edge of her pleasure, when from the corner of his eye he saw Julie and, without thinking, switched the focus of his camera onto her. For a brief moment, both of them were looking at each other through their respective lenses, each flashing a smile beneath the camera before nodding in acknowledgement and turning back to Angelica as she was pulling a satin pouch from beneath the pillows.

Earlier, she had mentioned to them that a secret admirer had sent her a gift wrapped in a necklace of pearls. The gift had been delivered to the hotel in the jeweler's signature light-blue packaging. She pulled it out again from the pouch, slowly now, and showed them the hard dildo. The pearls had been delicately laced around the shaft when she first opened the gift.

It had arrived with a note saying that the object was life-sized, and the pearls were from Japan, and that he would much appreciate seeing her wear both of them. Tonight, she was already wearing the pearls around her neck. They were glittering in the dim light as Jim saw her untie the side bow that kept her thong in place. With one hand she moved the fabric away, and with the other she brought the hard rubber cock to her mouth. He took another shot. Through the viewer, he could see the folded fabric of the polka-dot dress lying under her, framing her exposed beauty, the dots reminiscent of the gifted pearls and a prelude to the pearls of future fountains.

He got a shot of her mouth, lips distended by the girth of the object. And another shot of her pushing it, wet with saliva, further and further into her. With eyes looking straight at the camera and a hand holding the flat base of the fake cock, she moved to the rhythm of her awakened pelvis. The shaft felt so good, she thought, both in width and depth. No doubt she must meet him, that mysterious gift giver, she reflected as the smooth shaft slipped back out.

The camera caught the red lights from the chandelier reflected on the dildo. It also caught the polka dots, the pearls, and the row of her small teeth as she smiled widely, her head back, gradually finding the beginning of a trip to ecstasy where she knew all would be well. And safe. And nasty.

She took it all out. It looked so big on the camera, thought Jim. And then she put it back in, juices flowing down onto the valley of her ass. She was as open as a Botticelli Venus born from the seeds of the sea. She went faster with it, forgetting that they were there. Jim was taking still more pictures from a few steps away, and Julie, looking from a slight distance, wondering if she was going to do it. And then, with eyes closed and long moans, she did. She took it out and impaled herself slipping the full span of it within the shadows of her ass. She felt it fill her with the fullness of an unconceivable delight, mesmerized that she was the one doing it. Her cheeks spread open as she sat on it, the splendor of her pinkness front and center in the last picture he took before Julie gently dragged him out of the room.

As usual, they emptied their camera contents on the side table when they left the apartment, the music fading away behind them as they got closer to the elevator at the end of the carpeted hallway. Walking step in step, they remained silent until they reached the hotel's back exit to the busy side street and walked to J.G. Melons for hamburgers.

EIGHTEEN

JIM WOKE UP EARLY ON SATURDAY. Earlier than needed, earlier than expected. He stretched his long body along the bed, awakening his limbs in a lengthy yawn—his youth flowing from the core to the edge in one long tremor of pleasure, as if life itself had curled up within his chest during the night and now, in many rivers, was moving back through his solid frame. Like a feminine, almost feline, presence that regenerated his substance. Like the *Shekinah*, the feminine presence of God who comes to cover the world on the eve of Shabbat.

The trunk of his manhood rose as well, and he grabbed it. But today, in his empty bed, there was no one else to share it with. No one he could nudge, and tease, and rub himself against to feel his girth. No one to be the axis of a spinning sun.

Instead, he went to the kitchen, switched on the stove, and let his face hover above the heat of the blue flame. He loved doing that. He had been doing it ever since he was tall enough. He wanted to feel the artificial heat of the burning stove encompass his whole face at once. Like a thousand kisses. He lingered there just a bit longer until he placed a full pot of water over the flame for his weekend-morning eggs. He was thinking of Julie and how much fun it was to be with her, to laugh and live with her.

Yesterday, as they ate their burgers, "The best in town," she had told him, seated on the short side of a smooth L-shaped wooden counter, he realized how he constantly wanted to excel for her. Even now, while the two of them were sharing crispy fries from the same bowl and drinking from thick glass mugs, smiling and reminiscing about what they had just witnessed up there in the room at the Carlyle, he wished to impress her.

"What a crazy idea this guy had! She hasn't even *met* him yet!" she had said between bites.

"Yeah, crazy! But she was even more special by doing what she did."

"Yes, we do need these special ones."

"I wonder what she's doing now?" Jim had wondered out loud.

"Hm. . . . She's probably in her bathtub with the dildo

floating beside her, surrounded by bubbles."

"Like the Titanic." Jim smirked.

And, just like that, it had become their nickname for the mysterious lover. *The Titanic.*

NINETEEN

H E PUT TWO EGGS INTO THE BOILING WATER. Four minutes later, he rinsed them under cold water—a cold shower, like uncontrollable laughter during sex.

He sat at the kitchen table. Square and foldable, it had a yellow Formica top worn out by both age and use, with bits of its yellow surface missing. The gaps were shaped like islands or faces, and as he ate in silence, he looked at those shapes and found the faces he wanted to see. He even saw his brother, the one who had taken his own life and thereafter had come back to visit him as an oriole, red and friendly, friendlier than his brother had become at the end. He eclipsed that image with the first egg cup and started on the second one, eating slowly with a small plastic spoon.

The table, the shapes in the Formica, the spoon —all were echoes from decades before, when he loved home and ate at that same table.

He was not sure that his parents would condone what was most likely going to happen today. He and Julie were going back to the carriage house, back to the couple. He was unclear how he himself felt about it. But then the money was going to be very good. And he would do it as part of a team, with Julie by his side. Yeah, maybe that was what made him nervous, performing under the gaze of Julie and her camera.

He knew she would always keep his face out of the frame, and no one would ever know it was him. He had no tattoos, no ink that made him recognizable. Just a good body. A strong body that came from hard work in his youth, not just from visiting the gym, and that made a difference. He was the product of his life, not just its consequence. His form was following his function. And his function today was to perform in front of her.

He thought about Arthur's comment. How he should take care of both women. That was easier said than done. Arthur knew that. Arthur was still stuck back home with his high school sweetheart.

By now, it was lodged in Jim's mind, not just as his own fantasy, but his friend's as well. As if their combined wishes carried more weight, like layers of snow slowly weighing down his thoughts. One weightless snowflake of silent desire after another.

It was OK, he thought as he cleaned up the table. He could do it.

TWENTY

JULIE WAS IN THE SHOWER after her morning jog. She looked out the window and let the warm water run longer than usual on her long, muscular back. Maybe it's too muscular, she thought. But she could not help it, that was the way she was built. Long, lean, muscular. Henry had liked it, and that was all that really mattered. She kept it in shape in his memory. Like a gift for him to watch if there ever was an afterlife where you could still see things. She looked at the sky, her chin on the palm of her hand, her elbows on the ledge by the shampoo bottles. She looked through the condensed steam at a sudden, pink sunrise. Maybe there was a lens that could join both worlds—that of the departed ones, *Olam Ha-ba*, and ours, *Olam Ha-ze*. She smiled. Even if there was a lens, Henry had no more eyes to see with. No more lips to smile at her. Those lips surely almost gone by now, the flesh so thin that it would be like paper, like dust that would scatter. So how could he see her, how could he whisper to her?

At the end he had said, "It's time to go."

He had said, "I have come to the conclusion that it is time to go." She could say nothing to that. It was just too powerful coming from such a strong man. She had cried, and all the words she could have uttered that day she did by simply raising her thumb.

That was a long time ago now. And it was yesterday, too. The warm water was flowing over her hair, her body, and running along her legs when she made a fist with her right hand and, facing the new sun, once again she raised her thumb. It's OK, she thought, I can do this.

She was thinking about what she would wear later that day. She remembered the wife with her pleated navy-blue skirt. She could do that, she thought. A longer skirt, but in that style. Like a wink between women.

TWENTY-ONE

THEY WERE TO MEET FOR A LATE MORNING cup of coffee at a café called Via Quadronno on the Upper East Side, close to the couple's townhouse. The café was a world to itself, as distilled as its costly espresso. Waiting for her by the counter, Jim smiled at the women walking to the back of the narrow room, most likely for an early lunch among the ladies. A great spot for a professional gigolo, he thought. And then, he suddenly wondered if he too was nothing but paid pleasure, a tasty expensive sip. What the heck was he doing? he wondered. Was he sure of it? And then he remembered the beautiful woman in the house, and concluded, Yeah, why not? He would never have had her if it hadn't been for the circumstances, and boy, how he'd loved it then! With his eyes closed, he saw himself riding her again, his cock so hard with pure delight, pulsing rhythmically into the tender frame of her body. In and out of her at first, and then her delectable ass as well as she presented it to him. A target of so many surprises! He visualized once again how he had pulled on the belt wrapped around her neck and how it had brought her even closer. And how he had disappeared within her. He could see it all moving with the flow of an irresistible force, as old as the creation of the world itself, and so powerful that it was still present—right between his eyes at the counter of the fancy bar, with an empty cup in his hand. It was a force that would only end when all the waves stopped moving in all the oceans. The moon, he thought, must be from the moon. She was the one who moved the water, the one who makes us crave.

"What are you thinking of, cowboy?" asked Julie as she put her bag down at her feet next to him. "Am I on that train?"

He said nothing. He took her hand and, bringing it to his lips, he kissed it, his eyes in hers. It was a gesture of full abandon, of recognition, of possession, and of subservience. "I'll have an espresso, too," she told the waitress.

"Another one for me," he added. There it was—more money spent on a few tasty sips of coffee in ten minutes than he would have collected in a full day's work back at the farm, when he was a kid and they called him Jimmy. But there was value to this, he thought as he raised the heavy ceramic cup to his lips and felt the burn of the harsh drink slip into his mouth.

Value in the setting, in the weight of the cup, in the presence of all the other souls. He looked at her intently, focused on the red of her lips against the whiteness of the raised cup. She smiled at him, and they remained silent for a while longer. Content. Side by side at a counter. Partners.

"You ready?" he asked her.

"Ha! Are *you* ready?" she answered with a sweet laugh.

"Born ready! . . . I have something for you," he added, and from his pocket he pulled a small white package wrapped in a dark blue ribbon. He placed it on the counter next to her empty cup.

She looked up at him. "What is it?"

"Open it and you'll find out. It's not a dildo!" he added, mischief in his eyes.

"I sure hope so," she said, laughing, as she opened the small parcel. In the little box she found two pale earrings, silver with tourmaline stones.

"Wow! I *love* them!" She smiled at him. "But why?"

"I used the money we earned last time at the townhouse. No better use for it than to buy you jewelry, I figured."

"Hmmm. . .I will wear them now then," she said as she moved her head side to side and let the earrings playfully swing about. Little blue angels on swings.

They got to the front door and rang the bell. The red light of the security camera blinked, and the heavy metal door opened automatically. They walked in and the door closed behind them with a heavy thud. No one was there to greet them. They had expected the husband. They climbed the marble stairs to the main floor and found the same setup of dimmed lights and pulled curtains, and still no one. This time, though, there was a fire raging in the side corner where the sofa was, where Jim had joined with her the last time they were there.

They stood for a while at the entrance to the living room, bags of camera equipment in hand. And then Jim went to the fire and rearranged the logs to his liking. He squared the lower two with the long metal prongs and hoisted the third one perpendicularly on top.

"It's more of a man's job," said the voice. It was her. "I kind of like the idea that some tasks are for men and others for women. Even though it's not a popular thought these days," she added. The voice was soft and self-assured. It sounded clear above the din of the crackling wooden logs. He turned around, and in the glow of burning flames, he saw her. This time she was wearing silver pumps with heels and a long, shimmering pale blue velvet coat, like a gown, secured with large buttons and open at the collar. Her hair was up in a bun, accentuating the nakedness of her neck. He was taken by the sight, realizing once again how beautiful she was and almost stumbling on the memory of his previous encounter with her. It felt as if it had happened years before, if it had indeed happened at all. Mesmerized, he could only muster a smile, and then feeling he had to say something, "At your service."

Oh my God, he thought immediately, what a schmuck he was. *Here, at your service.* That was all he could come up with?

"I know," she replied in the sweetest voice. "And I'm much obliged." She turned toward Julie who was looking, on a nearby wall, at a framed black-and-white photograph of the bust of a naked woman. The image of that beautiful body had been manipulated: first it had been duplicated side by side and then almost defaced by wavy white lines—an erasure as much as an addition.

"Man Ray?" Julie asked.

"Yes!" answered the woman with a hint of respect. "Also called Emmanuel Radnitzky." She smiled.

"Yeah, Man Ray just sounds better," said Julie.

"It's funny how most times the artist's name has to fit the bill, even if they have to change it. There's power in the name alone."

They looked at the image together, the paired outlines on it mimicking theirs.

"It's a beautiful print," said Julie expertly, and she finally turned and smiled at the woman. A soft smile. One that came from far away. Soft and slow and powerful, like heat radiating out in a cold morning.

"I like your earrings," said the woman.

"They're a gift," said Julie, and without thinking glanced at Jim still standing by the fire. The woman instinctively knew, and Julie realized that she had been flagrant even without words, and quickly she added, "They match your outfit." She reached out and touched the soft fabric by the woman's shoulder.

Each gesture, each glance, worth their weight in words. Everything in the room felt somewhat artificial. The three of them alone, in a large luxurious space, dark in the middle of the day, with a fire fueling further heat on that warm afternoon.

Where was the husband? Was he coming? When do we start?

She knew that Jim had the same thoughts, but neither could verbalize them yet. It was just not the right time. And actually, Jim felt pretty good just standing there by the fire, with the heat layering itself over the front of his body like it used to do back in the country farm. A modulated heat that grew more intense when he got closer, his frame solid in the dancing light as he leaned forward.

Both women were looking at him now. All *three* actually, since the Man Ray model was also gazing in that direction. He remained oblivious, focused on thoughts from long ago when he sought refuge from a fire, the heat from the flames finding a deep layer that had always intended to remain hidden. He had to leave that place now. His spirit resurfaced, and he looked back up at them. Like a painting lit the right way, he was resplendent. It lasted long enough to imprint the air. Almost like the silver imprint of the photograph on the wall.

"Can I get you a drink?" the woman asked, breaking the silence. "I have Bellinis ready."

"Sure," said Julie.

"Sure," Jim said too, not knowing what those were but happy to oblige.

"My husband is out of town. A last-minute affair. But I did not want to stop our meeting today. I felt bad about it." And then, with a laugh, she added, "Actually, I kind of felt good about it."

She left the room, her heels making a faint noise on the thin Persian carpet and then a much more sonorous one on the hardwood to the open bar. She opened a small fridge, where three flutes were glowing in the electric light.

"Fresh peach juice," she smiled as she handed the drinks to Jim, who had come over to help. He added the champagne in each glass, and they all had a sip at the same time.

It was all so civilized, he thought, the bubbles an explosion of small kisses in the back of his mouth. He wanted to lean over and let it drip from his mouth into hers. Which one? he thought for a second.

Julie said, "Where do you want us to set up?"

"Here," said the woman, waving at the sofa close to the fire, "the same one as last time."

It struck Jim as the sexiest thing ever. That she could publicly refer to their "last time" at all was intensely sexy to him.

As if the words themselves contained the semen he had previously unloaded in the depths of her sweet ass. It was all too bizarre, yet here it was, it was all happening.

With their second Bellini in hand, they set up the tripod and put new film in the cameras. Julie adjusted the intensity of the lamps. Jim was starting to feel like a boxer getting ready to go in the ring, unsure though whether there was to be a bout at all. He rearranged the logs in the fire one more time. They would burn for a while, the fresh wood licked at by the older flames. Even the furniture seemed to fit the fireplace grate. He smiled to himself, looking at the Rateau chair beside the flames, unaware how rare that object really was.

He turned around to see the woman coming back toward the sofa, tray in hand, balancing a third round of cocktails. Her hair hanging long and loose over her shoulders, she shone dark and luminous in the glow of lights. Her open neck was like an invitation for all the light in the room to mold itself against her skin. In his mind, he undid the string of buttons and discovered her all over again. Slower this time. Slower, in order to remember it all that much better later. All around them the music permeated the space with a steady beat that spoke all languages.

He was fantasizing about what she might be wearing under the long jacket. Intermittently, he could see the glistening skin of her naked legs as she crossed the room, and he got as excited as a Victorian teenager. Whatever she did reveal contained such brazen sexual potential that he felt the need to drink more of her cool, sweet cocktail as a temporary respite from his overheated thoughts. His past desire for her streamed back into him like heavy wing flaps of a gorgeous butterfly. She was desire incarnate, not only because of her beauty, but also because of his past encounter with her—an encounter that only now, once back in the room, became fully elevated, as if he had to return to the scene to experience its full impact. Their lovemaking was somehow still woven somewhere in the substance of the surrounding air. He was feverishly waiting for her to sit again on the sofa, to gradually reveal herself and her nakedness, and then, looking up, to call upon him and ask him to join her in the flesh once again. He was ready for her, the heat of the fire on his back, the heat of the alcohol flowing in him.

Julie looked at him as she was setting the light intensity. For a brief instant, he looked at her. His body relaxed. He saw her. He saw how calm she was. She smiled and went back to the camera. He stood, waiting.

Maybe she knew already.

TWENTY-TWO

ER NAME WAS SHARI. She held a glass with one hand as she stripped with the other. Her hips were responding to the rhythm of the beat and, seemingly, his gaze. Her shoulders, like her hips, swayed side to side, and eventually the long garment slid to the ground without a sound. She wore nothing underneath other than a lacy balconette that cupped her breasts like two hands, and a pale blue thong matching her gown. Matching Julie's earrings. Matching Jim's eyes. Most likely matching even the sky behind the curtains.

On cue, the music changed tempo, the electronic beat as if originating from another stratosphere. And it was on that beat that she settled on the sofa, with both legs, raised by her heels, spread slightly apart. She was facing the camera. Facing Julie.

Facing, but not moving, as if waiting.

Julie started shooting, slowly, deliberately, taking her time as Shari, not moving now, looked intently into the lens as if she could see Julie's face through the body of the camera. Julie was using the Hasselblad that day, looking down on the clear, inverted image of Shari's beautiful body. Her nipples were raised just above the line of the fabric like pink berries waiting to be picked and eaten. She looked at the tonality of the skin on the screen and then, slowly and deliberately as well, let her gaze wander up, sliding along the edges of the vintage camera to better observe her—the open legs, the silent smile, the glimmer in the eyes locked upon her, completely oblivious to Jim. And when Shari, with two fingers of her left hand, waved for her to come closer, Julie instinctively knew what would happen next.

A long while ago, Julie had enjoyed the intimate touch of her Gyrotonic instructor. She even called on that vision, that sweet feeling, on nights when she was not quite ready to fall asleep yet, but that was it. She was through and through a man's woman. She loved their scent, their touch, their bodies. She had loved Henry's through all his tribulations. But she had not truly been herself since he left, and she saw herself almost mechanically take the few steps to close the gap between the camera on the tripod and the sofa. Like moving from one is-land to the next, swimming silently from one world to another. From photographer to potential actor.

"You were right. The earrings match!" said Shari, looking at her in the eyes while floating her hands up along her thighs, reaching high under her skirt, high into a twirl of seduction and unspoken desire.

Jim, bewildered, was holding on to his drink as if it were a solid pole and he could somehow lean against it. His eyes widened, his desire building up like steam billowing out from the New York City streets at night. He took another sip between his parched lips and then he realized, almost as a shock, that he should be taking pictures. He put the drink down on the mantlepiece and became the one looking at the inverted image on the camera screen. That was when he discovered Julie naked for the very first time. How appropriate, he thought as he watched Shari take the layers off. He was unable to take his eyes off the camera, fearful that it was only an illusion. Julie was even more beautiful than he had imagined her to be. Her long, muscular legs met her slender waist and shapely ass in perfect harmony. Her breasts were small but firm, with erect nipples under the hands that coveted them. Soon, lips joined for the longest of kisses. He watched Julie surrender to the life source being fed to her. Her hands eventually brought Shari's head closer, taking possession of her lips, and her tongue, and then the remainder of her body as the balance of energies flowed like sand dripping down an hourglass. She inhaled the full desire of Shari and let their mutual vitality merge into crevices of lips and tongues and diligent fingers of lust.

And then they were lying together on the sofa in a beautiful embrace of naked skin and linked limbs. He kept taking more shots.

For whom were they? he wondered. For Shari? For Julie? For him? He watched it unfold from within the confines of the camera until he saw the shot for what it was: an ephemeral imprint of liquid lust and desire frozen into artificial permanence. He saw in it all the other images of nudes he had looked at in books and in shows. He saw the rhythm of the nakedness filling the void, their bodies interlaced on the chocolate brown fabric of the sofa. He switched to black-and-white picture mode, and everything became vintage and almost unreal. Beyond the color of flesh. He kept looking at Julie as she placed her fingers deep into Shari, transforming the image on the screen into a faint blur as her hand moved faster.

Jim could not contain himself any longer. The time of being just a photographer was coming to an end. He did not know why he balanced his phone over the camera screen and pressed the video mode, but it did all get recorded. Much later, as if a dessert to be eaten only after a long meal, did he eventually see it all —from his nakedness as he got closer to Julie, who was looking up at him with the satisfaction of seeing what she had been hoping for. To his cock, which she brought to her mouth and made even harder before spreading Shari open and penetrating her with him. And he fulfilled her, and then Julie as well, whom he took from behind as she fed upon Shari, his belt resonating against the flesh of both women at once, stinging with joy rather than pain, while he went from orifice to fulfillment and back. Lips and digits followed the outline of a carnal passion, over and over, until they all had their fill and he finally heard the tremendous roar he bellowed out as he exploded onto both of them.

TWENTY-THREE

THE BRIGHT DAYLIGHT BLINDED Julie and Jim as they left the townhouse together. They were silent, as if reflecting on the brightness of the sun and everything that had just happened. She smiled at him as he moved her hair away from her eyes, and then the first available taxi took her home.

The three of them were making their way to their respective showers, almost as an act of sacred ritual cleansing. Different showers, but all with the same water that flowed, and healed, and renewed.

When you recite an individual prayer, you are supposed to do it silently, yet loud enough for your own ears to hear the words. For when you do that, you are one with yourself, as if within that loop little can interfere. And you are completely surrounded by words rather than visions or other thoughts. For Jim, it was a melody he sang in the shower stall, his body occupying almost all of the allocated space, soap lathered over his limbs, as he recited over and over, "I told you so. I told you, Arthur, it would be so. I told you so. I told you so." For Julie it was a short sentence she uttered only once, whispering into the steamed-up glass, "Wish you could have seen this, Henry," with an emphasis on his name, as if the magic of these letters would bring him back. She often did so after sex. As if what she had just done, just experienced, was intimately linked to his faraway world. As if it was a gift of sorts, or sacrifice, something that had a weight, like a lingering substance that traveled or like a taste of food. So was the effect of her love on souls long gone.

Shari's mantra in the hot water of her bubble bath was, "You told me to. You told me to." she repeated it enough times that it simply became "You, too." She paused. "You, too?" she questioned. "You two?" she asked herself again. And then with a laugh, she pulled out from the depths of the waters the beautifully smooth ivory tusk that had traveled from flesh to flesh as if an ornament to an ancient ritual. She brought it to her mouth, letting the hard surface bounce against the enamel of her white teeth and then deeper into the crimson depth of her memory as she saw his shaft once again, straight as an arrow, going deep into Julie and then deep into her. She saw, with her own eyes, the veins on his manhood as it disappeared ever deeper into her. She felt the ivory icon reach the back of her throat and tightened her lips upon it. A shiver started in her spine and traveled to the tips of her toes, surfacing at the end of the tub. She let her body tense up for a second longer and then released it all, the tusk plunging back in the water below the remaining bubbles.

She would look at the pictures later, after she rinsed off, she thought. And then she would decide if she wanted to show him, her husband.

She knew he would eventually like it. It was the new *zeitgeist* of the moment, a time when sharing was more than a fringe occupation. He told her that he wanted her to show off her pussy. Well, she had, she thought. He showed off his taste with his house, the stylish furniture, the elegant clothes. And now he also showed it off by exhibiting his wife. They all did. Showing off how beautiful their wives were. How good they looked in high fashion and high heels. How glowing the jewelry became on them. How well they moved after hours of training for it. He had just gone one step further and showed off how good she looked utterly naked. Almost better than with clothes on. He wanted to show her off.

And for others to enjoy her. Over and over.

TWENTY-FOUR

F OLLOWING THAT CRAZY INTERLUDE, Julie busied herself with paperwork, booking potential clients and
other stuff that kept her mind active and empty at once.
When evening finally arrived, she slowed down, letting the
transition from light to night happen within her as well. A
blanket of soothing darkness settled on her body just as it did
in the sky. And in that moment of quiet bliss, she realized that
she missed him. Missed Jim. "Mister Jim." She smiled.
Missed Her Jim.

He received her text message as he was drinking his first
cold beer while watching a football game on the sports bar TV.
He was wearing a navy-blue shirt, sleeves curled up as always.
At the other side of the bar, two girls were laughing, a colorful
cocktail in front of each. He had looked at them twice already,

a long look that could have meant something if they wanted it to, but they had ignored him. Or pretended to. Or maybe they had looked for an instant and then laughed some more. People were getting clumsy with nonverbal cues, he reflected. As most communication was digital nowadays, they were becoming less and less adept at reading body language. The faint art of telling without saying. Maybe they knew what an extra exclamation-point in a text message meant, but they were often clueless to the meaning of a single raised eyebrow, the beginning of a smile, a turn of the head.

His glance toward them had been somewhat predatory, that much he knew. He was horny. As if that morning had been an appetizer, though it had been a feast. He closed his eyes for a while, recapturing the visual impact of the women's flesh gleaming in the wavering light of the warm fire. Their bodies interlocked upside down, seeking out the depths of each other. And he, not believing his luck, going from one embrace to the next, plunging into flesh and further flesh, mouth, and more all at once.

He opened his eyes. Why was it that we had so many names for the female anatomy and just one for *mouth*? he thought with a smile. And in his mind, he saw himself stand up and go to the other side of the bar with his beer in hand and ask that very same question to the two girls. That's when he got the text message from Julie: *If you can, come over to my place. Now good.*

He looked at the two girls once more. It was always diffi-cult with two girls. You opened yourself to *witnessed* rejection in one scenario, and you most likely end up rejecting one of the girls in the other. He sent a thumbs-up icon and did not worry about the girls any longer. They probably wanted noth-ing from him anyway. Probably just wanted to chat at a sports bar, surrounded by guys. "Just chatting away," he murmured. He left a cash tip and walked straight to the exit, not even no-ticing how both girls instinctively checked his butt on his way out.

"I wanted to see you again," said Julie. "I mean. . .what happened this morning was so intense, and then ended so abruptly. And as much as I don't need to see her again, I wanted to see you, whom I work with. . . . And whom I care for," she added, a little slower. "I wanted to see you, and talk to you, before the night was over."

He listened, still standing in the living room, a glass of bourbon in his hand. He knew better than to talk back. Si-lence in these instances was always more productive, he had realized long ago. So she went on. She wished to be transpar-ent and open and trustworthy.

She kept on talking for a bit. Jim looked at her and was lis-tening, but he was also thinking. He felt a sudden pang of guilt and told himself that he had to delete that video he had taken. He would have done it right there and then had it not been a huge affront to be on his phone while she was talking about how good a team they were and what it meant to remain friends and business partners. And that they could split if it was an issue, but that she would never find someone like him, *et cetera, et cetera.* He just smiled, and occasionally he took a sip of his drink. She was right. It felt right to see her again the same day, not to discuss the future of Julie and Jim, but to make love again.

He looked at her lips as she spoke and, in his mind, remembered where these lips had been only hours ago. How insane was it, he thought, that you can perform the most incredibly daring sexual acts and look exactly the same moments later? There she was, Julie of the business, while she had been Julie of the lust storm in the morning. He put his drink down on a wooden counter and walked to her. He knew only one way to stop her from talking. He kissed the lips that had been wrapped around his cock and ravaging Shari a few heartbeats ago. And they were fresh and felt clean and virginal.

He pushed into her mouth a bit of the bourbon they were both drinking, like a foretaste, and she kissed him back, swallowing his amber gift and letting herself melt a little more into his arms. Happy to have him for herself now, now that the ice had broken and that what had to happen had happened.

He was to be her lover. And she was to be his.

And they would work during the day and fuck at night. And then she stopped thinking, because he spoke in her ear and said such sweet and nasty things that she could no longer hear herself think. And as in that prayer, he found her and brought her higher and higher. And she could only moan in response, her words swallowed by the essence of raw sex.

She grabbed his chest as he transported her, still impaled on him, into her bedroom and laid her down on the white sheets. She held on as he lifted her up further with each thrust, so deep that she thought she would faint. And she almost did as his hand grabbed her throat, and she left herself go dark and limp under him and for herself. And when blood came rushing back into her brain, she found herself again with the intensity that comes from the rediscovery of the world. The world and his cock that kept working hard and fast in her until he exploded once again, all over her naked face, so as not to spoil the clothes she still wore.

Instinctively, her tongue reached out over her lips. He tasted like an exotic fruit, sweetened by youth. He watched her fingers run along her face and collect some more and feed it to her open mouth. He helped her, tracing the outline of her lovely profile with the liquid seed. Her cheekbones, and her upper lip, her mouth closing itself on his laden fingers. Watching her throat move in the shadows of the room as she swallowed his essence, still in a dreamlike state as the trance slowly receded like a wave that leaves the crest of a beach. His fingers ran lightly along the edge of her skin and their combined scent lingering, ever so addictive, in the room and on their hands.

He kept the scent on his fingers, for he knew he was going to sleep there. He wanted to. He had never wanted it as much as now. He wanted to sleep there, in the bed where they had just owned each other, and snuggle with her and feel the weight of her body against his chest as he brought her closer. And as such they slept, finding refuge in each other's arms. Interlaced as old lovers, each unaware of anything but the welfare of the other. Expecting nothing else but the pleasure of that moment, they rested and skipped dinner until she found him again. But before he could drink from her one more time, she was up and twisted a robe around her body. "Come up," she said. "let's have a bite before the night's over." And she walked towards the kitchen. He stretched his body under the soft sheets, feeling vital energy flow to the end of each stretched limb and pool at the tips of his extended frame until it rejoined down to his core, where his muscles were still sore—the whole gesture, a reflection of his morning ritual.

He met her as she put the eggs into boiling water, his shirt open and loose over his jeans, top button undone, the base of his abdomen revealed. She ran her fingers along the coarseness of his southern hair, just long enough to get a rise from him, and just long enough for the boiling eggs to be ready.

They ate silently, dipping sliced toasted bread into the yolks. She watched as a golden yellow drop dripped along the rim of the egg holder bought so long ago. There was poetry in this slow journey of the pigmented seed, down along the curve of the shiny ceramic, as it urged itself to the tabletop, and further down, onto the Earth itself.

"Let's go to Fanelli's for a drink," she said.

TWENTY-FIVE

Back in her bedroom at the townhouse, Shari was resting on her bed. She had books and magazines scattered around her, legs tucked under the sheets, her imprint occupying a small space on the large bed. Finally, she reached for her computer, where she had downloaded all the photos from the morning session. She had waited a whole day before she even glanced at them. She had already wanted to do it a few times, but she made herself busy and got lost in time and in the house.

She found it special to have the whole house by herself for a few days. Her husband was out west on a business trip, and the kids had gone spring skiing. This did not happen often. "Not often enough," she said out loud, as she recalled the craziness that had occurred in the previous few hours. She'd also indulged in the serenity of the emptiness that surrounded her and even the empty kitchen, where she cooked for herself. She had absolutely been starving after they left. She'd cooked pasta with asparagus and lemon sauce and eaten it alone in the main dining room, drinking a beer straight from the bottle while reading the newspaper's style section. "That was almost as good as sex," she'd told herself, smiling as she looked up at a large Richard Prince joke painting that read, *I never had a penny to my name, so I changed my name.*

"I just received a text message from Shari," said Julie. "She wants to know if we have any images with you in them. She's under the impression that maybe it was recorded. She said she's hoping it was because her husband told her, "Loved the pictures, darling. But where is the guy?"

It had taken Shari a while to send the images to her husband. She had looked at them at length, letting each one impress upon her the weight of its significance, its debauchery. There were many and she'd gone on to delete most of them, distilling them down to a few that resonated even deeper— starting with the one of her with her legs open, looking straight at the camera. That picture, holding within it the full extent of what was to happen, she had sent first to her husband, awaiting his response before sending any more.

She recalled that he had asked for it, over and over, whenever they made love, and then again whispering the unmentionable request in her ears as he prepared to leave for the trip.

She knew the image to be a tease, but she needed to be sure that he really wanted to see more. The last time, he had been in the room with them when it happened. But now was different. He was far away. She did not want him to be jealous, though she had done everything he asked for.

She was good at choosing things. It was a gift. She knew how to pick her clothes without a personal buyer, the same way she knew how to select art and which branches to prune from the early spring limbs of her country trees. She had chosen a few special photos to send him, pictures of her and Julie, and tongues and flesh. She'd waited for his response, looking silently at the screen, and when he sent *Good job, honey! Send me more, my love*, she'd answered with a handful of selected shots. All at once, like a volley of arrows across the continent, the images of her deeds travelled electronically through thin air, as if on waves of unseen galloping white horses.

And then she had rested against the soft pillow. Her t-shirt had suddenly felt tight. She'd taken it off and marveled at her own nakedness, this body of hers, which had already done so much for one day and yet looked unharmed, like the beautiful painless birth of a flower. She'd caressed her skin lazily, not thinking about it, waiting for his response. His inflection.

The beauty of a fantasy lives through many stages. First and foremost, its inception, arising deep from within, followed by the feverish telling of it and the excited anticipation that stems from it. Then the retelling of it, which in most cases remains the final product, repeated as many times as needed. In rare instances, there is a performance of it. For fantasy is always a theater, a play, an act, an entertainment, a true performance. And as such, it can be extraordinarily wonderful, or it can be a total failure. And therein lies the fear that keeps most in the blessed safety of a world of anticipation alone. But if it does not fail, as she had not failed him, it opens up other worlds—the retelling of it, whether in words or pictures or sounds, and then later yet another retelling, over and over, and thereafter follows another anticipation when the retelling blends into further hopes for action. And perhaps the same. And perhaps more. So, goes the cycle that makes flowers bloom in the tree, if the tree is solid. If the tree is frail and the love is shallow, the apples will be born rotten, merging on the ground like dejected memories, seeds to no one.

'Tis but the same cycle that fuels the inner beasts.

She had waited to see, to feel, his reaction—his "digital reaction," she thought, in this new era of immediacy when answers sometimes preempt the questions. "Digital." She smiled, as she let her fingers remember the touch of Julie and she looked again at her phone. Julie was glorious in the picture she was looking at, her long muscular legs wrapped around Shari's waist in a most intimate embrace. That image was a far cry from Shari's daily routine and the strict, austere upbringing she had received, yet it was that very upbringing, being taught to be a good, obedient girl, that had allowed her to go from mere words of anticipation to the hard and tangible reality of today's acts. Looking at the pictures made her realize that she had finally done it, and she could also feel it deep within her. And strangely, ever so strangely, besides being so full and satiated, she also realized that she wanted *more*. Not later, when another opportunity would arise, but *now*. She actually wanted them back now. Both of them, Julie and Jim. She wanted them with her in this big bed where they could all play and sleep and take turns doing all as leisure would dictate. She wanted it to happen right here in the hallowed enclave of their bedroom. She had no doubts about it. Another inflection point, she thought, and they seemed to occur more and more frequently as the events unfolded. Desire spawns fantasy, and with fantasy grows desire, and sometimes that flower grows larger and larger, and may even overshadow the tree from which it was spawned, glowing brighter than the leaves and the sap from which it initially originated.

Her husband's query, *Where is the guy?* had precipitated the whole evening's events. Because of the weight of his words, sent all the way from another coast, the doorbell rang at the Upper East Side townhouse, and she pressed the entry button without even checking who it was. She was beyond checking by now. She had invited them back over, and she knew fully well who was at the door.

TWENTY-SIX

ARLIER, AS THEY WERE HAVING ANOTHER DRINK at Fanelli's, Julie had looked inquisitively at Jim after
reading him a text she had just received from Shari.
He had lowered his eyes just enough for her to understand that
there was indeed a recording—that he *had* secretly recorded the
morning's activities, and that he still had it in his possession.
Not something she would usually condone, but then again, the
whole thing had morphed beyond the scope of the usual.

We may have something, she texted back. *On our way to
show you.*

And to Jim, she said, "Are you ready for more action, cowboy? You may be called upon again." She laughed gently as
he said yes.

Everything happened soundlessly once they got into the

house. Jim made sure that the front door closed silently behind them, and they walked past the room where the smoldering fire still glowed in dying embers, and into the corridor to the bedroom. There a mellow light emanated from dimly lit translucent shells. Just enough light for a few good pictures, thought Julie as she entered, Jim following close by. No words were spoken. She, Julie, fixed the camera on the tripod, and Jim came around the bed, eyes fixed on Shari, steadily unbuttoning his plaid shirt. In silence still, Shari got up to her knees, displaying her black silk lace underwear. "Underwear is emotional," a friend had told her once, and she was right. This one called for bondage and submission. Jim's hand around her neck was a testament to this. She let the weight of her own head rest further into his outstretched fingers, a silent sign of acknowledgment to the growing affection she felt for him, and to what she really wanted him to do—like a seal of approval to the things she wanted done to her, recorded on film and camera, so that she could in turn send it to her expecting husband. It all seemed absurd, yet it made perfect sense at that moment.

And even later, as Julie took the shot of Jim's fully engorged cock penetrating her, her hands tied up to the headboard and the fabric of her thong pushed aside revealing her pussy dripping in delight, it still made perfect sense.

TWENTY-SEVEN

N L.A., SHARI'S HUSBAND CAME BACK from playing tennis. There, his day moved three hours later than his wife's, but in his mind, he was breathing the same New York City air that she floated in. He knew her to be a floater, at times. A passenger in life, as if surrounded by mist, she traveled the hours. Visible yet ever so gently separated and, at times, not even recollecting what may have happened in the recent past, she was a muse, an inspiration, a walking desire. Beautiful in stature, and shape, and skin, and with eyes that shone straight ahead towards the next step. And by God, had she taken the next step! he thought as he entered his hotel room. He had been able to glance at the images for a split second when he checked his messages while paying the tennis pro for an hour of play. He tried to remain calm in front of the guy, but he could see his own hands shaking as he handed him the cash. With a quick wave and a goodbye, he rushed back to his room. He rode up the elevator with strangers who had no idea what was in the phone he was holding ever so tightly in his hand. Even he wasn't sure of it yet, but he knew whatever it was, it was grand! And perhaps even great! He had seen blurs of naked skin, a blend of her skin and others'. He could not wait to look at it. He had nothing planned that night and was so relieved when he remembered he didn't. He had to remain calm. He had to make sure he was not going to die before he got to Room 518.

It was OK, he thought. The guys in the elevator did not seem like killers. There was a woman talking quietly about the evening plans she had with her husband, as if maybe the elevator ride was the only time she could have his undivided attention, or maybe it was her way of showing off the fact that they had plans together. She spoke fast, finishing each affirmation with a questioning tone.

He could not wait to get to the fifth floor. It seemed like he was on the local ride, with people getting off at each floor until he was left alone with the couple between floors four and five. Only then did the woman stop talking and looked at him, still sweating in his tennis outfit.

"Good game?" she asked, somewhere between polite and nosy.

"Oh, yes," he answered. And then could not resist adding,

"It's the after-game that's going to be great!"

They all got off at five, with the couple going right and him turning left towards 518. As he walked away, he heard the woman ask her companion, "What did he mean?" in her high-pitched voice.

He got into the room. He was still alive. He smiled. He would get to see these precious images before he died, he thought.

He had turned off the air conditioning before he left, and the room was pleasantly warm. Through the open window, he could hear distant birds speaking of love among the branches of the exotic trees. He sat down on the edge of the bed and looked outside for a moment longer, his entire being engulfed in a huge emotional wave. He wanted to savor every last minute of it. No one could stop him now. And nothing did. He scrolled through the images, feeding on them. He was like the oversized tropical leaf he could see outside, offering its full expanse to the blessing of the sun.

His hands shook now as he sat there, bringing the screen as close to his face as he could. He poured himself into the images as they gradually overflowed him. And in that screen, he lost himself in the love of his wife and the sacrifices she made for him. For his sake.

The images struck him like lights turning on in the distance. In the dark. Full of life and lust, he watched and tried to make sense of what she had sent from her phone. Yes, she had sacrificed herself for him and he could see the numerous digits interlocked along her skin—fiercely penetrating her in some images, and further spreading her and restraining her in others, allowing her thighs to be opened and be plowed. And through the magic of these pictures he saw, center and clear, the juices that flowed from her. An explosion of juices that made everything shiny and glowing, capturing even more light, and providing further certitude that she undoubtedly enjoyed satisfying him.

Even later, as he showered away the sweat and seeds, he still took the screen with him. Scrolling in the steam as he searched each image and video clip, he re-created in his mind the scenario that had unfolded in his own house, three time zones away.

TWENTY-EIGHT

MAYBE THE ONES WHO LIVE A BRIGHT LIFE, those who outshine even their own expectations, have to die earlier than most. These were Julie's thoughts in the very early morning, moments before sunrise, as she was setting up to shoot Angelica again. They were outside this time, and Julie had picked a spot she knew well from her morning runs. It was on the West Side, close to a small path sheltered by a huge, twisted tree. The patter of birds playing among the young buds and freshly unfurled spring leaves was the only real sound. The distant hum of the city was just that, distant. And reality itself was distant as well as Jim positioned Angelica the way Julie desired. Her hands bound up high around the lower branch, the fur-lined handcuffs visible around her slender wrists. She wore nothing else but a black silk outfit strapped thinly around her shoulders, with a deep and low cleavage that reached her pubis, the thong hiding her secret lips as the fabric arched back and linked itself above her buttocks to the sides of the garment. It was an ingenious twisting of lace and fabric that trapped her body and stretched in all the right places, revealing through the silk the outlines of her marble-like features. Julie smiled as she saw in a nearby tree the dance of two birds, recognizing their urgent quest for love, for sex.

"Ubiquitous." A solid word. She kept repeating it as she shot Angelica, with her high, dark green Prada heels resting on a bed of old leaves still covered by a thin layer of snow. The tip of the heels pierced the frost, her nipples as hard as ice. Angelica's breath was visible in the thin morning air. Julie had wanted her cold, before the sun rose up on her skin, and she had to time it right, for surely a crowd would gather soon, and someone would call the police. They always did in this country. They love to call the police as much as they love to hate them.

There was no one there yet. Jim pulled out a large reflecting blanket and hung it, partially hiding the naked body. Suddenly, the sun hit the whole scene at once. Angelica became visibly more and more uncomfortable, cold and hanging and strapped against the deep-seated tree. The light was magnificent. It shone all around them, seeming to coalesce on her alabaster skin as she stood there, imperial in her self-inflicted distress.

Julie nodded to Jim, and he moved forward towards her.

With a red silk ribbon, he blindfolded her. There was beauty in how he tied the ends of the ribbon with the ease of a man who did things with his hands. There was elegance in the way he flipped open his pocketknife and slowly let her feel the blade running along her skin as he cut the shoulder straps and let her top fall below her hips. Julie took the last shots. The sun glittered in the hard metal as it caressed the skin just above her luscious breast. She leaned forward onto it, now out of her control and comfort zone and in full view of the two joggers who came by every morning to pay respects to that tree.

TWENTY-NINE

BACK IN THE HOUSE, JULIE WAS LOST in thought even as she was busy working. On her dark wood Naka-shima desk stood the silent glittering screen of a laptop computer. On it, she was editing the last few pictures they had taken in the park. Angelica's photographs.

Instead of keeping them, Angelica had left the films with Julie. She wanted her to edit them and find in them a blend of strength and vulnerability. Vulnerability had been evident everywhere in the scene in the park—from her nakedness in public, with hands tied up high on the branch of the old tree, to the impact of the red blindfold in the cold morning air.

Strength, on the other hand, had emanated from her composure within the frame, legs crossed as if in tacit acquiescence, and from her smile, with lips spread wide, revealing the full extent of her pleasure. Julie was focusing on that smile. She wanted to make it front and center, the focal point of any gaze. She played with filters and depth of field controls until she felt she'd gotten it right. Using those settings, she worked on the very last shot. She recalled how the two joggers had immediately started to run towards Jim, and how she'd had to stop them by yelling, "Look! It's a *photo* shoot!" pointing to the reflective blanket deployed on the side.

"We mean no harm. Actually, please stand there together for one more second," she had asked. And then she had taken the last shot. The two runners seen from behind, facing Angelica—hands on the hips of one, and others by his sides. Their gaze focused on Angelica's face, her naked breasts, her overriding desire seen in the arching of her spine leaning forward against the restraints of her hands, and the brightness of her luminous flesh, absorbing the lust of the early morning sunshine. She looked like a divine apparition in the mist, a gift from Aphrodite—a gift she intended in her mind for the mysterious man who had sent the necklace a few days before.

Where does all this *lead* to? Julie thought as she was editing the photographs. Why this inherent attraction to sex? Should that time be spent studying instead, reading, writing? But was sex not all of these as well? she wondered. A study of the other and of the self, of reading the other's mind and body and writing nascent fantasies in the flesh?

She felt torn by it, lost in it, in her own body that at times wanted it so much and at others wanted never to even think of it. Lost in the thoughts of life without him, of her desire to get back to him, to show him, tears welled at the corner of her eyes, and her hands ran along the honed surface of the walnut wood of what had once been *his* desk—her fingers trembling slightly as the screen became more and more obscure and the tears dropped one by one onto the wooden surface. She did nothing to stop them. Did nothing to clean the teeny marks of their splashes on the wood, as if they were scars from the inner storm that often raged in her—a fragile link between the torrid sex and the overwhelming death. A body composed. A body decomposed. A memory that faded among the scent of the fragrant flowers she always kept in the room. Tuberoses today: Henry had loved them. They reminded him of Bali and the trip they had taken there together, where they'd listened to each other speak sweet words of love and tasted each other throughout the day. The scent of those flowers was like the fragrance of her pussy at night, he used to tell her.

She smiled among the waning tears—soon the crying would be over, and she would see the computer screen again, and she would work again. The impact of sex always there. Always the same. Never quite the same. It had the innate power to heal and to maim—always a gift to the precious moment, the instant, always insufficient in its plenitude. She was so confused. So close to call it home. And then she let the magic of her skilled fingers work the picture on the screen into a remarkable icon of cultural indecency.

Looking more carefully at it, she saw, partially hidden in the branches of the tree, nestled above the glitter of the metallic handcuffs and the blade of the knife, the discreet but unmistakable outline of a large bird of prey. A red-tailed hawk, she thought, its eyes apparently fixed, not on the tied-up Angelica, but straight at her as she was taking the shot. The voyeur observed. The ultimate, ironic serendipity! And she laughed outright. Her laughter rang where, moments earlier, there had been room only for tears. She stood up and stretched her body, releasing in waves what had been held inside. Feeling the pleasure of occupying the space that surrounded her, she suddenly began to think about Jim again. Where was he? she wondered. He must have brought Angelica back to the Carlyle. She knew that much. It was the right thing to do. Angelica must have been so cold, even after she put on the fur coat over her partially naked body. Who even wears fur nowadays? she had thought then. But somehow, the dark brown sheared mink coat looked like a natural fit on Angelica, as if certain objects belonged to certain people. As if they require a certain fit and we spend a lifetime searching for that fit in everything: in our friends, our clothes, our rings. And when it matches, it feels just right. Just like a knife fits in the hand of the chef and a brush in the artist's.

She was recollecting how he fit in her, his girth a source of constant pleasure.

Did he go back up to Angelica's room once he got to the hotel? And as quickly as the question arose, she already knew he had. How could he not? She could imagine how he ran a hot bath for her as she made tea for both of them. How, in front of him, Angelica must have slipped naked into the buoyant surface of the bubbles. How she made sure that the top of her breasts rose right above them. For she could not stop seducing, even when she was not conscious of it. She was seduction incarnate.

Julie was thinking about that, about them being so close to each other in the hotel bathroom. Of what a bubble that room was in itself. Within the suite. Within the large old hotel. Within this city of skyscrapers. And she realized she wanted to burst that bubble. To take a nail and not let "it" happen. Not let Jim slip with a broad smile into the soapy water and let Angelica warm herself even more along the strength of his muscles. She could imagine her reaching for Jim's cock. *My* cock, she thought. Angelica would surely grab it with two hands and mold it stiff with lust and warmth until it became so hard there was only one thing to do.

Julie shook her head. With that quick motion, she dispelled any thoughts and looked outside, where the immensity of the sky became a welcoming abode. In it she could get lost—in its color, its ubiquitous presence, and its absence of sense. It made no sense floating around the planet like a giant bubble, yet it kept us alive. It was always there, always would be, and as such it became the repository of all our aspirations, our dreams, and our dead.

Maybe, she thought, the thin, triangular molecular bond of ozone is a filter tight enough to hold the souls back. Like a giant net that captured them before they went frozen in outer space. And from that boundary, they returned to Earth, floating down like fallen leaves, aiming to populate a new body. A new anima. A steady rain of souls that ascended as fast as death released them and bounced right back into the fervor of fornication and the bodies that needed new life.

Then she realized she didn't care to think about it anymore. What she wanted was Jim. That was the simple, honest truth. She had grown fond of him, and now she was prey to that basic instinct—she realized she was jealous. She didn't want him over there, enjoying the luxury of a warm bath and Angelica's welcoming body. She wanted him *here*, wrapping his arms around her naked skin as she stood facing the sky. She wanted him to be here and hold her from behind and let his manhood grow between them so all she had to do was lean forward. With her eyes still fixed upon the immensity of the sky, she wanted to feel him fill her, his hands parting her legs, and his hips finally finding hers.

She touched herself. She was wet. Very. She *did* lean forward, as if he *were* there, as if she could feel his breath upon her neck. Oh, she wanted to feel him in her! Not only the full girth of his hard cock but also the weight of his balls bouncing against her pussy with each thrust of his fast hips. Let him have her. And if he slapped my ass, that would be great, too! she thought with another private smile—to the sky and all the possible souls ascending and descending, one of them perhaps still looking at her, floating in mid-air, looking at her mimicking being fucked for all the sky to see and for him to admire.

That was when her cellphone beeped. It was Jim. She knew it instantly because she wanted it so much to be him. It *better* be him, she thought. How sad if it isn't.

"I should install a special ringtone for him," she told herself as she walked back to the phone, barely dressed and unperturbed about possible glances from the neighbors. It was New York. She could do whatever she wanted.

"Thank goodness it was him!" She picked up the phone at once and saw that he had sent images. The first was a stupendous shot of Angelica naked under her fur coat, walking along a public path of the park. Her high heels extended her naked legs to a fulcrum of pure bliss and desire. Her feminine shapes were discernable with a hint of her navel showing and the collar of her coat laced along the fullness of her breasts. Her smile was still lined with makeup. Very vivid on video, thought Julie, but a good shot. Actually, a pretty great shot. Angelica could be clearly seen, the trees behind her, and a lonely jogger in the background, out of focus. She looked at it for a moment longer, eager to see the next image, but worried as well. The next image showed Angelica in her bathtub, exactly how

Julie had guessed, lying back on a surface of bubbles, the makeup dripping a little around her lower eyelids—her nipples right there, like islands amid the foam. She only glanced rapidly at that one. She did not need to look at it. She knew it all already.

She flipped to the third picture. To her surprise, it was a picture of her own hallway. She recognized the carpeted floor, the apartment number on the door, and she also thought the shoes, seen at the bottom of the screen, could be his. She flipped to the final shot. It was definitely him. His thick manhood sticking out of his unbuttoned pants, at level with her own doorknob, the bronze glow of the round knob a glimpse of how hard his cock could become.

She loved the way he spread her legs apart and slapped her —even before he entered her—noticing with a smile that she was leaning forward at the exact place she had been moments before, waiting now for the next slap of his hand, the extension of his pleasure, the sting of his lust.

Jim saw the black see-through fabric fall away on either side of her welcoming ass. With his phone, he recorded her cheeks becoming more and more crimson as she called for more and still more.

He was about to enter her, the wide head of his manhood already invading the image on his screen, when she turned around and his camera captured her on her knees, mouth as wide as she could, letting him slip into her. She looked up at him, saw the camera and did not stop. Her eyes locked with his. Her face locked in the same rhythm as his slow and deliberate thrusts. He put the camera down. He wanted more. Despite the incredible sight of her mouth dedicating itself to him, even taking him whole, he wanted more.

The camera now resting on the countertop, he placed his hands under her arms and lifted her up towards him and his full lips. She had tasted him, and she had loved it again and it was her turn to want more. His scent was like musk, like catnip.

That was when she realized that she was falling for him. Not just a bit, but head over heels. And she did not care. It was great to be in whatever version of love Nature was offering her these days. She jumped up to his hips, her legs tight around his muscular waist, and he placed her on top of the built-in unit by the window. Soon she found herself balancing on him, her arms outstretched like pillars behind her, his cock deep in her pussy as he moved in and out of her. Her midsection levitated in mid-air toward the safety of his core. Her mind scattered in a thousand pieces as the wave came over her. The city could fall apart. It could rip along its seams. The glass behind her could burst into a multitude of shards. Still, she would not care.

Let the souls see it all, if they could see at all.

"Don't stop!" she told Jim. "Don't stop!"

And he did not disobey.

For a long moment, she was transported. She could feel the long hair she no longer had on her naked shoulders. It was there. Undeniably so. Hanging heavy on her skin. Caressing her shoulders from behind while Jim faced her, here, on the ledge, near the spot where they used to sit together, drink tea, and then drink of each other.

The same spot. Different man. Same woman. And so different. Or was she? Was she not the same? Was Henry?

She was voracious, hungry for his touch, his words. Yes, but she loved Henry, and this was young Jim. Almost a toy. *I should not care,* she told herself, and she let her head lean back some more. Eyes closed. Enjoying her hair along the edge of her shoulder blades. And his cock, smooth and fervent between her legs. And then he spoke, and she had to will herself not to open her eyes so as not to shatter the illusion that it was *his* voice speaking winged words of love and desire to her.

When Henry was strong, he had always spoken to her. And now, and here, he was strong again. For both of them. She drank his voice and his scent. As if all of him was there. She kept her eyes closed a little longer. Why stop now? It felt so *delicious* being his woman once again, having him there in all his presence and tenderness.

The pain she felt along her outstretched arms paled in comparison to the delight that was running along her spine, out of her space and into his will. But she was relieved when, with her eyes still closed, she felt her body being lifted and placed over the table, a hand guiding her to double up face down. Her eyes shut even as she placed a hand on each buttock and spread them, revealing where she wanted him to go. There was no doubt in her mind that during all of this, during the time she floated away along his shaft, her long hair was really being pulled back in the manner she always used to like. No doubt at all.

Until later, when she woke up, snuggled against the warm and sweet-smelling body of Jim, who held her even in his sleep, and when, with her hand, she felt the back of her neck and her cropped hair. She smiled at him and let her face snuggle back onto the chest.

ACKNOWLEDGMENTS

Big thanks to Anouk, Gabrielle, Hugh, Rachel, Renée, Gabriel, and Scott. And special thanks to Kite and Barry.

·

www.ingramcontent.com/pod-product-compliance
Lightning Source LLC
Chambersburg PA
CBHW041606240626
47164CB00009B/194